A Short Sad Book

A SHORT SAD BOOK

a novel by George Bowering

Talonbooks, Vancouver, 1977

copyright © 1977 George Bowering

published with assistance from the Canada Council

Talonbooks
201 1019 East Cordova
Vancouver
British Columbia V6A 1M8
Canada

This book was typeset by Beverly Matsu at George Payerle Ltd., designed by David Robinson and printed by Hemlock Printers for Talonbooks.

First printing: September 1977

Canadian Cataloguing in Publication Data

Bowering, George, 1935-
   A short sad book

ISBN 0-88922-127-8

I. Title.
~~PS8503.094S56~~   C813'.5'4   C77-002196-4
~~PR9199.3~~

"Under our gaze, the simple gesture of holding out our hand becomes bizarre, clumsy; the words we hear ourselves speaking suddenly sound false; the time of our minds is no longer that of the clocks; & the style of a novel, in its turn, can no longer be innocent."

Alain Robbe-Grillet (1954)

Dear Reader Reading:

1. Please take your time.
2. Also there is one dream in the following pages.
   You should be able to find it.

This book is dedicated to Old Port Tipped Cigarillos & Murchie's coffee, without whose help it would not have been written.

Various chapters have been publisht in the following publications: *Longhouse,* edited by Wm. Scharfe; *NMFG,* edited by Gordon Lockhead; *Is,* edited by Victor Coleman & Linda McCartney; *Iron,* edited by Paul De Barros; *The Malahat Review,* edited by Linda Sandler; a symposium for George Woodcock, edited by William H. New; *Center,* edited by Carol Bergé; *The Story So Far,* edited by bp Nichol; *Periodics,* edited by Paul De Barros & Daphne Marlatt.

A SHORT SAD BOOK

PART ONE:
Canadian Geography

Chapter I

I was going to write a book about love, & one time I woke up & said I love this country.

I was dreaming of what I saw in New Brunswick, several small boys with old haircuts, sides & back shaved up, plaid shirts. I remember sadly, my town boys lookt like that.

Thirty years ago, they dont anymore.

I love this country, I didnt then, thirty years ago.

I didnt say I did.

I didnt wake up from a dream saying that, I wrote that, it was something like a dream.

When I grew up I was going to be an American boy. I loved that country. That was human nature not my mind.

I didnt say hello to my mind till I came back to Vancouver from the east fifteen years later.

I was going to write a curious book about love, that was my dream but that wasnt either, I just wrote that.

Hot damn, I did it again.

I love this country I was going to write.

Do you know I am keeping secrets from you & I want you to discover them. & I will be disappointed with myself if you do.

Let me introduce myself.

I am eight years old & my name is George Bowering & I will change that & the name of my country when I grow up.

I will shoot the guns out of their hands the way all us Americans do.

These are not difficult ideas these are not really ideas I have just wakened up. Number one is waking up.

Number two isnt even an idea. It is the second little boy in New Brunswick, his name is probably Alec & somebody loves him. Enough to cut his hair he is a Canadian.

I remember him. He lived next door to the sawmill in Lawrence. I am going to call this book a novel. A love story.

Between Fredericton & Moncton there is a Gulf station, that is what I was dreaming about. It is just exactly like the one in Abbotsford but not the one in Lawrence.

16

Chapter II

I dont like to see stakes holding up the peonies. No I dont like to see them & I dont like to have them.

I told her this & she says she agrees with me, she doesnt like to see the stakes either but she doesnt really agree with me, not the same way. I mean the way I dont want them to rebuild the barracks in Nova Scotia.

Dont let the weeds grow but let the weather work & tell us how.

What is the use of having peonies if you have to support them. We are & we have done the same.

In Calgary they burn down the old buildings or they move them to the museum park. I wish they did not move them, that is worse than burning them.

Love. I love an old grey shafthead in the mountains & probably bits of iron hooping around the ground.

I dont want them to move it or recycle it or paint names on it. I dont want them to preserve it. Taking a photograph is all right, that is not preserving it that is making a picture.

I took a shovel to the ground where Fairview used to be but I didnt find any complete bottles just millions of pieces. Somebody broke them. I hope the great Fairview fire broke them.

I would love it if the fire broke them, but I would also love to have a complete bottle. All I would do is wash the dirt off.

That is just like a haircut. Come to think of it I went with my shovel just after getting a haircut.

Do you see why that is just like a haircut. I hope you do. I would love it if you do.

I was going to write this country I love.
You can write with a pen with purple ink.
You can write with a shovel.
You cant write with a blueprint for restoring Fort Dream. No you cant.

I love earthquakes & I love peonies but I can never learn to live with stakes to hold them up.
With crutches for my grand-dad but not stakes for the flowers.
I can agree with that. But only me.

Chapter III

No we never shot the guns out of their hands, we didnt even have guns.

Except in the War in Europe & not as neat as their guns either kind of English & fuzzy scratchy uniforms bulky bad-fitting uniforms where theirs were sleek.

& flat helmets like English air-raid helmets first world war helmets & they had that beautiful American helmet I told you about, the chinstraps always loose dangling & holding your hat on when you dived for shelter.

Our soldiers always had their chinstraps done up, those flat tin hats would fall off if you were just walking across a field.

Dug but not planted. The war.

No we certainly didnt shoot the guns out of their hands. In the war their guys had square automatic pistols with a clip like Dick Tracy.

But if our guys had pistols they were long revolvers like Mountie guns & fastened to them with a cord.

We lookt just like Englishmen how embarrassing.

I was going to talk about the Star Weekly when I started.

Where our drawings werent as good as their drawings in the Saturday Evening Post. I never saw the Saturday Evening Post on Saturday, we were nowhere that was going to happen, maybe back east in America.

In the war in the Star Weekly we had the Union Jack & I had to carry the Union Jack in a parade & there up on a pole was the Stars & Stripes Forever how beautiful.

We had gas masks & they didnt have gas masks, how did I get back to the war I wanted to tell the story of the Star Weekly it was something that came to us & told us that back east in Ontario they had barns with silos & white fences & hockey.

I always wondered what hockey lookt like no I didnt it was the still pictures in black & white of the Carr brothers & Foster Hewitt's voice from Watrous. I never thought about what it lookt like a hockey game. I loved it & I knew it stopt when guys were offside but I didnt know what offside lookt like.

I knew what it lookt like when they shot the guns out of their hands. The Lone Ranger was in the Star Weekly.

Chapter IV

In the North they dont say South or down south, they say out. When they are in the north they say out. They have been out or they are going out.

In the South we dont say the south but we say up north. Sometimes in the north they say down north. The river flows but you can drive over the line & not see the line & you do & you dont. We have all been & done the same.

Would you like a picture of the north. It is just as you imagined, it is in the north.

We say back east & back east they say down east & back east & down east they say out west. But along the St. Lawrence river they go north, not down north but north, & they say they are going east.

When you step out of your apartment in Montreal you begin walking east but you have to remember to call it south, I almost forgot right now, if you are talking to someone from or in Montreal.

This is if you are from out west or rather the west coast. In the east, as they say on the radio, they say the west coast if you are no longer in Alberta. They think all the mountains are the Rockies.

We dont know each other very well. Or we have to learn our way we have to get our directions.

In the north it is true, the moss grows on the north side of the tree, just the way they told us in the school books from back east. This was not true out home on the west coast up in the mountains.

In the north in Inuvik they told me they get out for a while & then they want to go back, into the north.

Now I know, airplanes make it in.

They make it in the north, that is they make it be in the north.

They make it in if the weather is okay.

They make it out the same way.

In jail you are in or out but getting out isnt getting out of jail, not in the north, whoever thought of that some Toronto editor.

In the north they dont like Toronto editors, they always say the papers down south come out & are filled with malediction for the real north. Bad words flow from bad blood.

If, I think, you can go down south & from the same place you can go down north you must be on top of the world.

They dont wear helmets up there they wear baseball caps.

Chapter V

Scenery has no beginning & no end. It has no ending. It is there everywhere whether you are there moving or still or not, sorry David Hume.

I mean sorry David Hume I usually am your champion but on this I am not, I know that scenery is always there whether you are there or not.

A pair of plums may be eaten two one nothing or left in the refrigerator to decay. A line of trees, well you cant eat them but you can drive by & the trees never end & never begin, you do.

For our purposes scenery begins from what you can see standing on the beach at Sooke Inlet looking west but it doesnt.

I saw a line of trees at Naramata British Columbia & then when I moved I saw a diagonal line of trees. From the air it was a rug of trees.

But I had to get up there by machine, so much

for the subjective. Scenery has no beginning or ending but you have & I have & my dog has & even airplanes have.

I saw a stand of trees in London Ontario where Walt Whitman the American had walkt & we lived a block away.

He said he had no ending.

Well, here I am Walt, & I dont see you around & you still havent annex'd Cuba & Kanada.

Scenery has no beginning & ending but Canada does. Standing in the water up to your ankles at Sable Island looking east.

The right side of my brain says scenery has no beginning & no ending but the left side of my brain says Canada starts at B & ends at d.

I'm writing this with the left side of my brain but I'm trying to see with the right side of my brain.

What do you mean, this is no novel.

Novels have a beginning a middle & an end. But scenery doesnt.

Chapter VI

Well yes when de Soto was weighted with sand & dropt into the river he was eaten by love eaten by revenge eaten by a fish as big as a hog eaten by Her, eaten to disappear into the maw of desire, to disappear never again to be seen by the eyes of men.

But someone I dont know falls off a boat & lies for days in Lake Athabaska. A grey lake & up he comes again & there is broken beer bottle glass all over the Canadian Shield.

Fish but no revenge.
No snow white.
No sleeping beauty.
No alpine clitoris waiting to spring.
No warm cleft in the wide tree. No, Brian.
No, Peggy.

Fish but no thwarted love in Great Slave Lake.

I saw them walking in over their heads together fully clothed into the river, this was before they straightened the river, & they loved one another they didnt care particularly about the river.

The best young swimmer in town drowned right there at that spot, he was sitting on a kitchen chair in the river, a true story, & simply fell off & drowned in the river.

Two years later another true story the best skater in town disappeared under the ice in the lake & he came up again & it was simply another lake, smaller now & really they told us a back-up from the river.

Some years the lake was under the ice but "Canada" wasnt & you two werent.
You dont have to be spooky to fall in love.
& you don't have to be spooky to drop dead.

What about the novel, then, is it all plot & scenery & no theme?

Oh I love you he said I have waited all my life for you I have watcht you sleeping & woke you with a kiss you should be more careful with needles you should always wash fruit before eating it. I was sent here & I have been waiting for you all winter, all my life.

No you havent she said.

Chapter VII

The whole country is beneath me when I bend over like this to write it. Bending slightly he flickt a wrist shot.

It wasnt the whole country then it was in Toronto Montreal New York Boston Chicago Detroit but most of all Toronto, on the radio from Watrous. That is said my Dad in Saskatchewan. I knew he was born in Alberta he was a great ball-player & basketball player & badminton player & track star.

But no hockey.

But hockey. Our national game he said on the radio though some more political people even then said lacrosse but that was in a textbook or back east & here we never saw anyone play either it was baseball, versus Grand Coulee.

Not really versus, you understand what I'm saying. It's us against them even now & us includes

Grand Coulee Tonasket Oroville Omak Penticton Kelowna Princeton Lawrence.

That is I knew the smell of diamond dust but not the gas of the ice in a rink. A rink, Maple Leaf Gardens was what was said between mountain bursts of static but not as exciting as look sharp da da Da da da every October.

So of the two what a choice, I was afraid to play baseball with others but I had no choice about hockey. I heard him say offside but I didnt see it I just said oh good but I knew less about how it lookt than the name of the street outside Maple Leaf Gardens. I didnt imagine there was a street there & when I saw it years later I was shockt but when I walkt thru the gate into Fenway Park I knew just where to go.

Are you surprised this is so clear? I'm writing about young love. I once masturbated into a baseball glove.

When Bill Barilko's plane was finally found in the Ontario bush I had no idea what the country lookt like.

Now it is all beneath me when I bend over to look at it this way.
It is extremely clear.
I am lucid tonight.

I am writing with the clarity of regret.
The Red Sox lost the fifth game today.

Chapter VIII

They say we are like them & I used to think we are like them & if we are like them how come we arent them how come they arent us. This is a patriotic novel. It is set on the battlefield, they kept coming & we kept pushing them back.

They invaded Quebec they invaded Montreal they invaded Niagara we shot one of their pigs in the San Juan Islands they said we have come to liberate you Frenchies you can practice speaking American, bombs bursting in air, they said non, merci, some of our volleyball players said we are like them when the Mexicans taunted them on the court, Whitman said we will add Cuba & Kanada, Jefferson said we will stretch from the equator to the pole.

It is true, we have to find out what we are not first.

We are not first.

In Mexico we were not even second.

Cuba was second.

I found out I was not American first.

Long before that I knew I was not British & I thought I must be American.

I listened to KING & lickt the backside of George the sixth.

I was always embarrast about the king on the stamp, the king on the money, the Union Jack on the flagpole, the English accents of all the piano teachers.

I was thrown out of school for walking across the gym floor to have a drink of water while they played God Save the King on a phonograph after the sock hop, this was spring of 1952, Stan Musial was going to repeat as National League batting champion.

This is getting so personal, it has to be a short story, novels arent that personal.

This is an argument about structure.

No an argument about form.

Hurray for Claire Trevor.

Thru the dark cold & the empty desolation, the wave cry, the wind cry, the vast waters, came my 1952 sweetheart, OGGE plus some numbers, on her ID bracelet, it could have been upon a torn-off arm, she came out of the blitz to save me, October

10, 1952, & then when I found out what I was not fifteen years later she was living down there as if we were like them.

He sailed out of what might have been to what had always been & the bombs rearranged the architecture.

She told me once, 1956, you are not James Dean & I thought she was stupid but I knew she was right, behind my horn rim sunglasses I knew she was right.

She was right.

She was a lost lover in a patriotic novel.

Chapter IX

In Ottawa two days ago I saw a human shape slumpt against the wall across from the National Art Gallery & I wondered is he alive or is he art. A uniformed guard took a look at him.

He was so big he was a cop. He could break his bones to make his living. That is what cops do & that is what Ontario does. It is almost human nature.

The shape lay with his feet straight out & his hat tipt over his chest not a hat but a parka hood. He was a figure on the ground.

So he must have been art all right.

(I walkt up to him & tipt up his face. It was Gabriel Dumont. Where is your mother I said. He said the last time I saw her she was in the basement doing the laundry.

He had been in love because it was a novel. We are & we have done the same.

His eyes were sharp on the edges. He only

wanted to sleep in the warm air. He really did. I let his head tip down again & he was David McFadden.)

I went into the National Art Gallery, out of control & in the first person. I was surrounded. They took my package

(& they took all my clothes. Walk naked into history they said. Paul Kane came thru a door to my left, riding swathed in buckskin & serge on a brown horse with long mane hanging one side, head down a foot in front of the other.
He waved pathetically, a paint brush in his hand. Have you seen Art he askt. Have you seen Canada.
It must be around here somewhere I replied. He rode his pony to the edge of a cliff, awaiting command).

I returned to the elevator in my hotel. There was a man fifty years old, his chin shaved in spots his hair sticking out his coat hanging from his arm to the ground a folded newspaper ragged in his hand & he was carrying a carton of milk.
You dont look like a Liberal I said. I feel like one he replied.

(I watcht him get off at the Ground floor & walk out the front door. He gave Gabriel Dumont a wide berth.
Dumont was not a ship. He did not feel like

36

one.)

The women with me were interested in Art & Canada. One was from Binghampton New York. One was from Johannesburg.

I felt as if the background of the novel was beginning to take shape.

Chapter X

I had no idea what the country lookt like. "They used to think that the world was there as we see it," she said. "But this is not so the world is there as it is." What an accident, what dialogue, & that is what a novel needs. Scenery & dialogue. I think she was right when she said a play was just like landscape.

People appear in it & do something.

Well I said it is a novel & so I will at last give you some scenery & dialogue.

She stood in front of a tree & she stood in front of a tree & she stood in front of a tree & she stood in front of a tree & she stood oh you poor typesetter in front of a tree & she said.

"We are Acadians & you want to send us to Louisiana & we will never see a beaver again," & she stood there in front of a tree.

"Well your heads are whatever vegetables you

prefer to call them," he said.

"You got that out of a book," she replied.

"Yes," he confest. "History is us."

"History is us, too."

"Perhaps," he smiled. "But history is written by winners." He moved between her & the tree. "& I will write this book."

She lookt past him to the tree. She knew it would be cut down after she went to Louisiana, & made into paper & the paper used to make a book.

"Will you remember me in your book?" she implored.

"I will remember you & all your comrades," he said soberly.

"Perhaps you will call your book Evangeline," she suggested, for that was her pen-name.

"No, I have the title already chosen," he mumbled.

"What is it?" she murmered.

"The Tercentenary History of Canada, Volume II, From Champlain to Laurier, MDCVIII — MCMVIII," he announced. "It will be publisht by P.F. Collier & Son."

So it was that the axemen of Acadia set to work on the scenery & converted it into dialog. The novel grew & Acadia grew more bare, till they began to plant apple trees in rows. Yes they did.

PART TWO:
The Exile of Evangeline

Chapter XI

I did not know where I was going but I was on my way I was going & I knew that because I was going. We are & we have done the same & so have you.

I might be hiding things from you but I am hiding them in this book.

At least you know where to look.

I wish you luck.

I wish you good luck & I wish you bad luck.

A little treatise on snow.

In Fredericton you cant look out your window across the street because the snow is piled half as high as an elm tree.

They say Canada has a frozen heart, a heart made of ice, kept hard all summer like under sawdust. They say her breath is terrible & she will track you thru the forest & snap your body into pieces & eat them.

For this reason we have invented the snowmobile. It is the triumph of the machine over obvious mythology.

I jumpt into my snowmobile & drove thru the empty streets of Montreal. A snowball came out of the dark & burst into a thousand white pieces against my headlamp.

It may have been bicultural sex but in the dark I couldnt tell.

That is the real meaning of snow in Canada.

Snow is always connected with the dark & snow is always connected with bicultural sex. Think back on your own experience & you will agree. Only in this way is snow truly Canadian.

I lay down in the snow in Westmount Park & made an angel. When I stood at her feet she was speaking French. She was just my size all thru the cold weather. Al Purdy went by without a word. He was speechless or it was too cold. When he wrote about sex & death it was nearly all death.

The angel said vous avez done a truly biculturelle acte. I was dizzy with gratitude, & attempted to become more oblique, more obscure, more distant & more unapproachable.

I tried to turn this short story into roman-à-clef.

If I had been someone else I could have told where I was going by the tracks, at least until it started snowing again.

Chapter XII

Try to think hard & try to imagine or really try to remember, try hard to picture it if you can remember, & in fact forget imagine & remember remember: have you ever seen a beaver. Remember this is prose have you ever seen a beaver.

I am trying & I cant quite remember & I'm afraid I imagine.

Remember is really for a short story. But one wants to remember, even in a novel. But if you remember in a novel you make believe you have imagined. You make them agree that this is a novel & not remembering.

It is hard to imagine finally & really for someone who has not lost a member.

I disremember, they said in my grandfather's time & now really in your great grandfather's time you'll have to imagine. I dont remember, we say now, I dont. I dont do it, not as a habit.

There was nearly always a beaver on the five cent piece & sometimes a beaver on the stamp, on pale blue with a garnet coloured edge. The nickle had no milled edge, the beaver makes a dam. He tinkers with the flow.

I have seen pictures of beavers, I have fake memories of beavers, Carleton McNaughton walking rubber boots out of the swamp with a beaver by the tail in each hand.

I also confuse maple leaves with the other leaves lying in my garden.

I have certainly seen an eagle I have seen a bear I have seen a snake I have seen a lion shaking his tail at flies in a San Francisco zoo.

But have I seen a beaver. Where are they, back in Ontario where the maple leaves & silos are & where they really do say "aboot," where the maple syrup is where Barbara Ann Scott was where the Happy Gang got paid once a month?

Where the early explorers walkt in snowshoes & took the clothes off every animal that lived in that country?

Have you decided yet whether you have ever seen a beaver not counting the one you rub with your thumb.

They used to come up with their trucks & snowshoes & square guns & ask us where they can find the nearest moose. They never even mentioned a beaver.

I always told them be careful where you walk, the rattlesnakes are mean on an overcast day like today.

In 1971 I finally saw a moose. It was standing on highway 17.

Chapter XIII

Remember who Flycatcher was in Lament for the Makers & you will be off the track, where invention happens. Look up invention. None of us novelists has a patent on that.

Evangeline packt up her few possessions & got on the train never to see her homeland again. The train pusht west, into Upper Canada, & then out, as they say, west.

The CPR was the first railroad & the CNR was the second railroad & that has nothing at all to do with history. I grew up in Lawrence near the spur line that brought an apple train twice a week & it said CPR on the side & when I went to the Coast it was on the CPR. In Ontario the CPR is a country cousin.

I often saw tumbleweeds in the cow catcher

because they were on the track.

A white rabbit is the house that Jack built.

I saw them in frock coats & spade beards driving the last spike. Nailing the country together.

Evangeline sat impatiently in the club car, waiting to get thru the mountains. She couldnt wait. She was an easterner & the mountains scared her. She said if she lived there she would chop them down, preparing the setting for a great Canadian novel.

It is a problem in perspective said her creative writing teacher.

You stand at the rear platform of the train & watch the parallel rails meeting at the horizon, but in the mountains there is no horizon just rocks & American hunters who have run out of Jim Beam.

This is turning into a picaresque novel.

Evangeline thought about perspective & decided to switch into the third person & Van Horne pulled a switch & handed out Christmas bonuses to the Chinese gandy-dancers.

This is getting altogether too dense for the beginning of a novel said her creative writing teacher. You're supposed to be offering an opening exposition.

A white rabbit scurried across the tracks & the chapter she had been composing ran away from her, just as the whistle blew.

British Columbia was welcomed into Confederation & the prairies were doomed to fiction.

Chapter XIV

I love this country, I didnt the thirty years ago but am I I. A poet is not a dealer in a card game. Not even a poet writing a novel.

They all do in this country.

I held her & kist her right on James Bay. For a moment she wriggled in my grasp.

That didnt go very well. In that case was I I too much.

The snow covers me & I lie covered with snow. Is it the grasp of winter. Is winter my country.

My country it is not a country it is winter. We all stood & sang that in the Forum. Where the sun never shines.

Brian skulkt thru the trees looking for his love. In the shadows. In the pines.

I cant remember when I first saw a maple tree.

It was in a zoo, behind bars. Driven into its trunk was the last spike. When I pulled it out I was not ready for the spurt of maple syrup. Brian would have been ready. He would have stuck his thing in.

But Brian is not I he is the other & she is too.

I am I because my little tree knows me, he said, grasping her trunk with his bare arms.

Only God can make a tree I thought.
So what am I. Doing here.
I am literally writing this novel on recycled paper. That is okay, recycle paper but not gold mines.
Contient des fibres désencrées et recyclées. Mon pays c'est l'hiver.
Mon cher.

I kist her in the middle of Lake Superior.
If I am I that is no way to find out.
The active voice & the first person.
Confuse setting & person confuse landscape & characters & you wind up with thematic criticism not a novel.
Anthropology not fiction.

You're right I never kist her at all not even when I finally crost the border at Waterton Lake.

I hesitated for a moment there & that did it I was definitely I.

To hell with the first person he was definitely he. When the snow fell in earnest he was definitely him & later still indefinitely.

Chapter XV

She stept off the train in the middle of Saskatchewan. Steam around her feet puft grey & billowed into the darkness. It was so cold in the winter black it seemed to fall cold from the dome of black sky. There the ten thousand stars were clear, they barely blinkt, they belonged to the cold black Canadian prairie night. She walkt along the platform & the comprest snow squeakt under her thin black leather boots. When she breathed she could feel frost in the hairs of her nostrils, the air cut a hole of ice into the back of her throat. She felt very Canadian for the first time. She could feel the cold attacking the fronts of her thighs even thru the three petticoats. No, not attacking, it was the air here, it belonged, it was here every year. The light from the windows pickt out the light powdery snow. She watcht a plume of snow blow off the corner of the roof up & into the light from the green-visored bulb on the pole. To the west a dark bank of cloud was blotting out the stars. It seemed low, it could have been reacht by humans, it could reach humans, she couldnt in truth see the low massive cloud but she knew it was there because the stars were not. When she blinkt her eyelashes lay frozen shut for part of a second. She felt the cold air now on the insides of her thighs. A tuft of brown couch grass stuck out of the snow. The snow was nearly as light as air, or the air was heavy as snow. The dark frozen earth stretcht from here to Baffin Island.

A mile away a cow stood with its tongue frozen to an abandoned harvester.

Three miles away a farm woman clencht her buttocks, afraid to go out to the privy.

Inside the station a sparrow hopt from the back of one bench to another.

The train suddenly bumpt & banged from the front to the back end.

She turned & walkt back to the train. She would be able to sleep now. For the first time she had been at home in the middle of Canada. They had told her about Canada.

She would always want to come back & visit for a day in the middle of the winter.

This would always be Canada for her.

For those who lived here it was not by any means Canada. It was Saskatchewan.

Chapter XVI

From the corner of my eye, this instant, I can see, while I write these words, a huge inquisitive reptile head at my window, looking in. I can get up carefully & escape by way of the door on the other side of the room but then what. If this has happened more is bound to happen. & why is this book changing so much.

After thinking for a while & reading for a while & indeed reading & thinking about my wife's reading about thinking & I didnt mean to go that far but there it was maybe the poor creature wanted to be let in on the writing, because this was happening in my writing room & you know what windows are in writing.

Now was that thinking or was that writing.
Or was that thinking or was that words.
Or is that were those words.

Or is that are they were those words.
Or is this thinking after all.

You want to write about the country you live in & this is what happens.
I wouldnt feel so bad if this wasnt a novel.

So maybe that was the country after all saying for heaven's sake let me in, quit putting in stuff about philosophy.
& if that were a character speaking I would say what philosophy if you think that is philosophy you've got the brain of a dinosaur.

My favourite place in Alberta (oh this new pen is getting broken in nicely) is Drumheller (my wife will hate that one because she hates this novel she says I'm getting too far removed from my readers with all this obscure self-absorption. What do you think dear friend) although I have been there only once.

(I mean I said it was a novel but did it say it was a novel. & if it didnt say so it can hardly be a novel because then it would have been something else calling itself a novel & I would have disagreed.)

It may get to be a short sad book.

What I meant to tell you anyway is that Drumheller is where the dinosaurs come from.

You can go there & see them any time you want.

    & that is how one's writing gets all tangled up with the country one comes to love.

Chapter XVII

It is so if it is written. Even if we are fresh & wet & not even half there. Even if we are.

The maple leaf forever. We used to sing that song & it was just like the barns & silos just like Jerry's father at the office, things I had never seen. Your father told you about things you had never seen because he was an adult. & the same with Canada. It told you to sing about things you had never seen. What did a maple leaf look like.

You learned to draw one, what is this second person doing here, oh, I see now, just as you learned to draw Australia, it was hard at first but the more you did it over & over the easier it got. A maple leaf.

There were not many trees with leaves on them. Some of the well-off people in old & big houses had them. Maybe one was a maple leaf tree.

Thirty-five years later I have a tree outside the window of this room & I think it might be a maple tree. But it might not.

If they were serious about making us grow up & become Canadians they should have sent us a maple leaf.

Besides, I got it mixt up with the maypole dance, short pants, 78 RPM whoooosh da da dee da da, da da dee dum dum.

I'll bet, I thought, those beavers gnaw on those maple leaf trees.

We had Dresden China, or someone did within hearing.

It is so if it is written.

Eventually you get a cheque for a hundred & twenty-five dollars & you're still writing it. If you hear this it's happening again.

Charles G.D. Roberts got up from where he had been lying & there was a yellow-brown maple leaf stuck to the back of his sweater, now we're going.

Why do the Leafs wear blue & white sweaters. I always wondered. I didnt think blue was possible, even back east or in a text book.

He folded his little volume of poetry, a leaf prest in the middle of Tantramar, & walkt back toward sleepy Ottawa. Confederation was beginning to deepen in the western sky.

The maple leaf forever, he thought.

Calice tabernac watch where you're going said a beaver among the mat of leaves on the forest floor. Watch where you're going, are you dreaming or something.

I made that up & now it's there. How are you going to unmake it. This is an adult book.

Furthermore sorry, he said, a kind man. He had seen too many animals die. They died of exposure.

No it's not there, it's here.

Forever.

Chapter XVIII

I have been all over the country save Newfoundland & I have never come anywhere again. & neither has anyone else. No images please. Or if anyone else has why has she. There's something wrong if you come anywhere again, it means you are not in the country at all. You are in your mind, here we go again David Hume.

This book is about Canada, it is not in my mind. My mind is in Canada.

A few drops of my sweat are in Lake Erie.

When I get to Newfoundland it will be new terrain. In the middle of a sea.

If Evangeline finally got to Vancouver she was there & there is nothing you can do about it.

A Cajun in a motorized pirogue, looking up & saying just yesterday arent the mountains beautiful.

Yesterday I said to my daughter look at the new snow on the mountains & she said of course. I said why of course & she said because they need new snow to look like mountains. Another true story.

True is new & new is true. That is tradition. Do you know what mountains are.

So Evangeline met John A. Macdonald in Vancouver, he was resting up from driving the last spike. She said arent the mountains beautiful. He replied would you like me to take you up there.
Is winter my country she said.
& up they went.
Neither of them had a bottle.
There were no American poets along.
The rest belongs to history.
Do you read me?

I have been to Acadia once & when I go to Acadia I will not come there again & neither will you.

It's in speaking that ideas come to us, words, & then we, in our own words, we find perhaps everything, the city too, the garden, & then we are orphans no longer.

When they got to the top of the mountain John A. Macdonald put his arm around Evangeline

& said it appears that you have become the central character of this novel & if you will look down you can see the Fraser River & Burrard Inlet. Someday this will be all yours, my love, if you but say the word.

"Merde," she said.

Far to the east she could see a train arriving on the CPR tracks. It was filled with Scotch & Irish immigrants.

Chapter XIX

What it means to be a Canadian.
It doesnt mean anything to be a Canadian.
When I was six I said what bad luck to be born part of the one-eleventh who were not Americans, & later I said what good luck to be among the one-ʼleventh who were not Americans.
They have nicer helmets & smoother uniforms that's all.

No it doesnt mean anything to be a Canadian.
Nobody can shoot the guns out of their hands, not even us.
If my grandfather had stayed in England would I be an Englishman. If my other grandfather had stayed in Missouri would I be an American. Dont be silly. Something else would have happened.

The only part of Canada that looks like it was

designed is Saskatchewan. There's meaning for you. A straight line here, another straight line here, a third straight line here, a fourth straight line here. There you are. Saskatchewan is defined as something in the middle of four other things it is not.

Maybe I mean it means nothing to be a Canadian.

I'm having trouble with this. Is it a political novel or a philosophical novel. If my grandfather had stayed in Missouri I still would have read "Evangeline" but I would not have read A Short Sad Book.

My grandfather stared ahead of him. The Canadian prairie lookt a little like the American prairie. His constant singing Indian companion said it means nothing to me.

But where are you from askt my grandfather Emmett.

I am not from, said his companion. I am here, at your side. My bones denounce the buckboard's bounce.

Dont engage me in ontological sophistry, said my grandfather. I'm from Missouri.

I dont get the allusion, white man, said the Indian. Indians get sore bones like anyone else.

Yes, but what do you do with them when you're finisht with them, said Emmett.

The novel was beginning to get serious, like the conversational part of a D.H. Lawrence book.

My other grandfather passt D.H. Lawrence every day on his way to the mine. He never recognized him & no words ever passt between them.

D.H. Lawrence wondered who was the other lad with red hair & why was he so sunk into silence.

Later one of them moved to Canada & the other moved to the United States. Neither of them considered what it meant to be anything but English. It didnt mean anything.

PART THREE:
Canadian History

Chapter XX

– Did your mate send you a fortune?

– No! Only some photographs & papers about a place out there in British Columbia.

– Would you go there?

– I thought perhaps we might.

– Oh yes! I believe it's lovely!

– The postman is gone now lass, let me get on with it. This is position one. No, legs a little higher. Eh! What it is to touch thee!

– Oh that's easy, like rolling off a log. Dont they have lots of logs in British Columbia?

– Ay, lass. Now turn around. I'll show thee position two.

– Oh lovely, yes, I feel the dictates of biology. This is turning into a dirty chapter. In any case, since it is the fault of this large *thing* & not your own fault, you can neither be blamed for your position nor be expected to do anything about it.

– It is not.

– Oh dont stop moving. It is not what?

– It is not a dirty chapter. Judge Bryan declared it a novel of "rare beauty & literary merit."

– Do they have beavers in British Columbia? I dont believe I have ever seen a beaver. This is getting to be dirtier & dirtier & I cant help it. It is beginning to parody itself.

– Nay, if yer want to I'll move thy pretty arse to position three.

– Oh yes, look what's being done to me. It isnt fate, is it? I am making a decision. Let us go to that place.

— Evangeline, this little room is everywhere. Speak to me not of British Columbia now. F dash dash K the British. Darn Columbus.

– My name is not Evangeline. I am going to assume position four.

– How do you know position four? 'Appen I am your teacher.

– You have to assume position four in a wheelchair. You have to be a creative non-virgin.

All this dialogue was too much for the novel. I noticed that it was beginning to speak in short sentences with periods.

Literature fell from the skies.

The novel withdrew itself painfully from its skin & assumed position five.

The skies opened.

The queen of England smiled. Her face was green. On her back a road in Saskatchewan ran to the distant horizon.

The army of adjectives mounted an attack upon pure prose.

The garrison held for three seconds.

The queen smiled upon her red children.

If you are not Evangeline, who are you, askt the red-haired man.

Chapter XXI

Canada is the country in which writing about history is history.

Let me try again.

I meant to say that Canada is the country in which writing history is history.

In some countries killing natives is history & in some countries killing kings is history but in Canada writing history is history.

Every historian writing history knows this.

Every historian is aware of this, he is at his desk writing history & he is the history of Canada. He is the history of Canada in many volumes.

It might also be true of literary criticism. It might be true that Canada is the country in which writing about literary criticism is literary criticism.

We will never know for sure. It is not part of history. In Canada history is writing about history.

For example Lester B. Pearson did not go down

in history until he wrote history. Then he was part of history.

In France they took time off from writing history to kill the king & became the high point in French history.

In Canada they wouldnt have had a chance. Napoleon would be a nobody here.

In Canada the only history is in the history books where it happened. Nobody ever does anything about it, they write history & enter history.

Do you doubt it. Dont doubt it.

When Hitler burnt the books everyone in Canada was angry. No one will ever believe it they said. & they were right. Ask anyone born after the war in Canada, do they know about it.

In Canada if you want to be a great figure in history write about history.

It is not very exciting but it is history.

The less people read history the less history there will be, I see you're back, David Hume.

That is obvious isnt it, the less people read history the less history there will be.

This is true of Canada.

But not of the USA. There they will kill presidents & have more history than they know what to do with.

Have you ever heard of a Canadian prime

minister being killed. Of course you havent. It would not be history.

In Canada the only history is writing history. That is a matter of history & this is Canada.

That is why in Canada geography is all over the place & history is in the history books.

Chapter XXII

Now I cant help thinking who was the first Canadian, someone had to be the first Canadian. If once there were no Canadians & now there are twenty-three million Canadians, sometime there had to be the first Canadian. Either that or there are still no Canadians. Then who is wearing those red sweaters at the world hockey tournament.

Now was that thinking or was that writing or was that history.

The Asians who walkt across the Bering Sea & became Indians if they did were not Canadians, they were Asians just as you are a Canadian if you take a plane to Isla de Mujeres & just as your children will be Mexicans if they stay there but first they will be just your children.

When they are one year old, this is not anthropology this is psychology, when they are

one year old you can ask them their nationality &
they cant tell you. So there are only twenty-two
million Canadians.

Thank you again, David Hume.

That reminds me, first all the Canadian explorers were French & then they were Scotch.

I can tell you the same thing about Lief the
Lucky. He was not a Canadian, he was lucky.

Cartier was in Canadian history but he was not
any more a Canadian than Ernest Hemingway was
a Spaniard. You cant even say Hemingway in
Spanish. Hemingway is not in Spanish literature
but Cartier is in Canadian history.

That is why in Canada the only history is
writing history.

Captain George Vancouver has a city & an
island in Canada but he has a city in the United
States & a rock in Australia & an arm in New
Zealand & a mountain in Alaska.

No, Captain Vancouver was not the first
Canadian.

When they invented Upper Canada did the
people call themselves Upper Canadians.

Maybe Confederation invented the first Canadian, but before Confederation the Americans
said those Canadians.

Let us say 1835, it is 1835 & you are now all
Canadians. Some will say no I am British, I just live

here & my sister lives in Britain.

But it strikes me that everyone is now a Canadian. How did all these Canadians get here.

I guess I became a Canadian when I could read the stamps. They said Canada. But what would have happened if I couldnt read.

If I couldnt read I wouldnt be able to write & if I couldnt write I would not be able to write this history, & if I couldnt write history there would be no history, not right now.

That is why this is a Canadian historical novel.

Chapter XXIII

I should never have tried to be classical because I come from the mountains.

The mountains are romantic by nature. In the mountains is romantic by nature.

Canadian history becomes romantic when you get to the mountains. The same is true of Canadian geography. There is no Canadian geography. There is lots of Canadian history. More every day. They are writing it at a university near the Great Lakes.

In the mountains with the Acadian girl, John A. Macdonald felt all at once very romantic. He pickt some alpine flowers & offered them to her in his trembling fist.

The flowers are nice, she said. But I would rather have the earth they grew in.

But this land is promist to Macmillan-Bloe-del, he said. Everything over a thousand feet to

Macmillan-Bloedel, everything under a thousand feet to the CPR.

Who is Bloedel, she enquired.

I wish you hadnt askt me that, he said. I dont know, but I can assure you that he is a part of the national policy.

It sounds to me like a classic rip-off, was her reply.

I'm afraid you will eventually end up in Louisiana, my dear. Come, let us go down now. I just have time to catch my train.

You couldnt catch a cold, she thought to herself. Theirs was a love-hate relationship.

Yes, Canadian history becomes romantic when you get to the mountains.

Back on the flat lands they tried to be romantic but it didnt work. When Louis Riel stood up there was nothing to hide him from the bullets, the country was too flat.

All you can do in flat country is run. The mountains are for hiding. The flat land is for running. This is not geography, it is history.

I am writing it & what can you do about it.

In the novel Romantic Riel stood up & held the cross high & said "Flacons de blé!"

A bullet snipt the top off the cross. It became a T. Louis lookt at it & pronounced it a sign. T stands for Toronto, where the Orange Men live, & their power is stronger than the Church, he said.

Power comes from the muzzle of a gun, said Toronto. A thousand Chinese gandy-dancers nodded, their hands tuckt into the opposite sleeves.

Superstitious Louis went to Montana, which signifies mountain in another Romance language.
Evangeline went to Louisiana.
John A. Macdonald went to Scotland.
D.H. Lawrence went to New Mexico.
Captain Vancouver went to Hawaii.

It made no difference to Canadian history.
Canadian history is writing Canadian history.

Chapter XXIV

The early explorers had to hang around until Canadian history opened. It opened at ten in the morning. They were anxious to sock away their animal clothes in their savings accounts.

Riel was himself romantic & he is dead not by & by but dead. Quotation is something like history. It is writing history.

If you follow my thought like string at the end you will run out of string.
I have completed miles & miles & miles of air travel, I know.

The young woman poet said in Montreal, if you do not find out a lot about your subject how can it be a novel. Like Hugh Hood how can it be a novel.
The novel knows all about it but I dont I said.

Not in quotation marks but I said it.

She lookt around for help. Nobody would help her.

The novel is writing it, I said, trying to help. I only get afraid when I try to help the novel, but to help the reader that is all right. After the novel.

But I thought the novel was a character in the story she said. At least once in a while.

Yes, I suppose so, it is at heart an auto-biographical novel, I said.

I had said the novel died in 1950.

But if you arent writing it & the novel died in 1950 how did all this get here she wondered.

How did the first Canadian get here, I responded, being first reader of the novel.

Fuck that she said, causing embarrassment all round. She had none of my insecurity about my nationality & none of her own.

The ghost of the novel is writing it, I exclaimed, that is why he knows so much more than I do, & that is why the novel can have a chapter about someone who does not believe in it.

I dont believe in ghosts she said.

Well what can you do I said, it is a ghost-written novel & I have already made a thousand dollars from it & more if you are hearing this.

It would be a romance if Riel was really dead but only if he were writing it & then it would be in French & then it would be a roman & that is a novel.

Riel is not a historical figure he is a character

in a romance, out there where he belongs, frant-
ically trying to make a mountain out of a mole hill.

That is what novelists do.

But not novels.

Novels are the news.

John A. Macdonald read the news on the train
east.

Riel was dead again.

Chapter XXV

If I lie around here on the beach long enough the whole country will run down. Weeds will grow in the cracks of Confederation Centre. The novel will give up, shrug its shoulders & walk away into the Gatineau Hills never to be see again.

It'll get eaten up by a bear never seen by the eyes of an Idaho marksman.

"Emotional entropy is simultaneously a cultural & personal predicament."

Job offers are nothing to sneeze at.

I'm allergic to sand anyway.

But romantic you know romantic if anything is romantic there will be something dead in the neighbourhood.

Romance has a great need for death.

In the Eighteenth Century nobody ever died, they just went on making social errors.

There was no Canadian literature in the

Eighteenth Century. Check & see. No Canadian literature in the Eighteenth Century.

As for Canadian history in the Eighteenth Century, well Canadian history is writing Canadian history. Yes he is.

You can watch him doing it at a university near the St Lawrence Seaway.

I may be romantic but I am no dream & I am sometimes a victim & sometimes not. I am a victim in the morning when it is already afternoon on Bay Street. The Vancouver stock exchange opens by Toronto time.

I am never a victim at night. At night there are lots of shadows & lots of romance & lots of death.

The death of Montcalm took place in full sunshine in the Eighteenth Century. No one noticed in Canada or in Europe.

The death of Montcalm & the death of Wolfe were classical in nature.

They are the most important paintings in Canadian history.

Wolfe wore red silk & Montcalm wore blue silk & both wore white wigs. Everyone in Canada knows this.

I have never seen a beaver dying but I have seen Montcalm dying.

It was his own fault.

If I lie around on the beach long enough I can

see the clouds take on the shape of the death of Montcalm.

A few minutes later & they will be puppy dogs & bunnies.

If I wait long enough they may look a little like a beaver. Nickles may rain from the sky.

If I dont get up & do something the whole country will run down, including the Globe & Mail, Toronto's national newspaper.

Back in Toronto the clouds take on the shape of barns with silos.

Chapter XXVI

General Wolfe's bullet went thru the brain of a dray horse & continued west over Lake of the Woods until it passt thru the body of Evangeline, making a ninety degree turn at her left hipbone.

You have performed a truly bicultural act, said the angel, & Wolfe lay back dying hardly able to bear leaving the new world once called New France where he had not been around long enough to see a beaver. In Scotland he was so busy killing hillbillies he had not had time to see a haggis.

In days of yore.

In days of yore Evangeline was going to die of love, old & American, not a stray bullet from some bushwack hunter drunk on Johnnie Walker.

You learn it in writing poetry you tell it in writing prose.

She had no choice, we have all done & been

the same, she had no choice but to go down there & be just like them, eventually, dead as all get out.

Just as I was going to write a curious book about love, I have the reminder pinned to my wall, the bullet came out of Evangeline & entered a beaver, it came out of the beaver & entered Big Bear, it came out of Big Bear & entered the Carr brothers, it came out of the Carr brothers & entered Lee Harvey Oswald.

Now that's interesting.

Lee Harvey Oswald has just entered Canadian history. With a bang.

You cant do anything about that & neither can I & neither can the Central Intelligence Agency. They arent paying for this book.

Knowing look in Ottawa.

The bullet came out of Lee Harvey Oswald & expended itself in Lake Huron. It may lie on either side of the international boundary.

My mother is outside the door right now wondering what I'm hurting my fingers for.

It is human nature.

I was going to say the Dragon Lady, thinking of that reptile Canadian history or was it Canadian literature trying to get in, everything is trying to get in, now you see Terry & the Pirates trying to get in.

They were in the Star Weekly. No Wunder.

    I'm probably not hiding anything from you at all.

    & no she isnt that she isnt the Dragon Lady not by any means, maybe that means I'm trying to get in.

    Maybe that means this is prose.

    It is a military novel about General Wolfe who died & got into Canadian History some time later.

Chapter XXVII

Mr Crump, have you seen a bright lily grow before rude hands have toucht it. Have you markt the fall of the snow before the soil has smudged it. The snow white lily lies under an abandoned musket on the plains of Abe. Have you felt the wool of beaver, or swan's down ever, or smelt of the brier's bud or the nard in the fire, have you tasted the bag of the bee. Oh so white, oh so soft, oh so sweet is she.

Mac, forget her, she left on a stretcher for the Gulf of Mexico.

Yes Mac, forget her, this is poem containing history, not a bloody romance.

You have no sense of tradition, you just want

to lay track thru the sump, Crump.

Tradition is the rhythm working thru history, said the railroad baron. Or somebody. Donald Davie, if you want to know the truth.

You have the advantage over me because the CPR has a beginning middle & end but Canada doesnt.

You are the first Canadian, Mac, so it does have a beginning. It is a classic case of Confederation.

I am a Scot, I drink Scotch whiskey. I go out to the end of the railroad & find a stone carved by Alexander Mackenzie. I find a bottle thrown overboard by Archibald Menzies, I'm in a frenzie.

You're getting drunk, Mac. If you dont straighten up we'll have to set you off the train at Piapot, Saskatchewan.

Where that lunatic redskin keeps holding up the train?

We just give him a couple of Hudson's Bay blankets & a few boxes of shells & he lets us go on our way, said the Baron.

But he'll use those bullets to shoot holes in the National Policy, said Mac, listing a little to starboard.

Out the window he saw a cow with its tongue frozen to a harvester.

You're just gun-shy since that spent slug made a hole in your sweetie-pie, Mac.

It could have got me if it had bounced off her other hip, pal.

The train passt Piapot without incident. Incidents are not history. Writing history is history.

He'll use those bullets to shoot holes in the National Dream, Mac persisted.

He tries that & his life wont be worth a plugged nickle, said the Baron.

You're thinking of the wrong country again, said his messy-haired drinking buddy.

Right now my country is summer, said the Baron. I'm going to build a railroad to Costa Rica.

I'm going to build a historical novel & fill it with the names of hockey players. If Hugh Hood can do it so can I.

Isnt that a Scotch name, askt the black porter on his way to the dining car.

Chapter XXVIII

I woke up out of a curious dream & said I love this country.

But.

I was going to say but something. But something made me say but. That was all. Now she will really hate this part.

You were just getting going on the narrative & you had to fuck it up with this.

A lovely rime I will say.

That sounds better than I thought it would. I wonder if history is written that way, if it sounds better than they thought it would.

American history looks better than they thought it would. But American history is not writing history. Not even with an American dollar pen. No, Miss.

No I.

No S.S.

No I.

No peepee.

No sir, no I.

Not any more.

I was going to change the name of my country when I grew up but now I'm not. Just the town I was born in & why.

Charles G.D. Roberts pusht his way thru the deep snow, on his way to the railroad station. He reflected upon how the Americans had forced Canadian history to happen now in the west. Van Horne hung our hopes on the last spike.

Evangeline wrote him a letter from the bayou. She said you have your hangups & I have mine.

Charles G.D. Roberts wrote ten patriotic poems about the snow. The snow was also his garden now. A victory garden.

Reading Evangeline, he was filled with envy. He changed the name of his country. They publisht his stories in Boston.

By golly, said the dean of arts at Harvard. That man is making history up there.

History means something to say, said Sir Charles.

That's a special view of history, said the dean of arts.

That's your American brahmin perspective, said Sir Charles. I'm talking about roots.

There's nothing wrong with his perspective,

said Van Horne. I would have put the rails thru Montana if that drunk Scotchman hadnt gotten wind of it.

That was human nature, not his mind.

History has no beginning or end it is all middle. What has an end. The rope Romantic Louis depends from. The forty-ninth parallel that seeps into the water at White Rock.

Not even that, it goes round & round.

& what makes that happen.

Love.

Love & history are different names for each other.

That's why I love writing the short sad history of this country.

Chapter XXIX

A chapter about the relationship of time & history.

There is no relationship between time & history.

There is lots of time. It goes on & on. Dont worry there is lots of time. Just look at it anywhere & you'll see. There is so much time no one has ever seen more than a little of it.

But history. There is only so much history. History has a beginning middle & end. It ends when someone angrily throws his typewriter into Lake Ontario.

The history of Canada is all about the Great Lakes & sometimes the St Lawrence Seaway.

Who did what to whom happened in time.

History is all about writing history.

All about.

History is all about.

One is in time.

History is all about.
Just have a look.

When John A. Macdonald got back to Kingston he declared the BNA act. The BNA act said that French Canadians could speak their language but they couldnt grow bananas.

John A. Macdonald didnt want any republics here especially no banana republics. Hence the BNA act.

In a sense he was making history.

One day he was standing in the park in Kingston reading a letter from his lost love. It bore a Louisiana postmark & was written in French.

It was a simple message. Just a crude drawing of a black hand.

John A. moved the capital to Ottawa.

In the winter it was the coldest city ever to be a capital. In the summer it had more repellent insects than any capital city in the northern hemisphere.

They'll never get me here, he thought.

He was a Presbyterian & felt guilty about drinking.

Ottawa declared repressive drinking laws. They were called the blue laws because John A. Macdonald had the conscience of a conservative. His autobiography is on the fiction shelf in Edmonton.

Lee Harvey Oswald was cold stone sober when he shot John A. Macdonald.

It never got into the history books & you know why.

The novel said you havent been around for a long time, do you still think you know where you're going.

Yes I said but I cant get Evangeline off my mind. Frank Basil Tracy told me in confidence that her head has an uncanny resemblance to a turnip.

There you go again said the novelist's wife.

It's a matter of history.

You could look it up, he said.

Chapter XXX

George Bowering sat at his desk writing history. The usual phrase was writing poetry & that was the word he had to correct in black ink. He watcht it happening under his very eyes.

He wondered what to do at times. He could leave the page blank down to there where the clever remark is but he wanted to give the people their words' worth.

Or if not that their Bliss Carmen.

He sat at his desk & wrote history. What he wrote was George Bowering sat at his desk writing history. He didnt make the mistake, so something is playing games with history here.

Maybe it is poetry.

Now there are two desks, the one he is sitting at writing history & the one in history.

Unable to get in the door, his mother stept over the windowsill. He only imagined this the way he imagined Canadian literature.

You have very eyes, she said.

Thank you, he replied.

That was the clever remark.

He returned to writing history. What he wrote this time was you guesst it George Bowering sat at his desk writing history. What he wrote was George Bowering sat at his desk writing history. What he wrote was history & you know why.

He was filled with more energy than usual. That morning he had sat at his table eating Quaker Oats & reading the Quaker Oats box. What he read was not of historical interest but it was something like history.

His friend Lionel was fascinated with Lee Harvey Oswald on television. He had watcht Lee Harvey Oswald die on television one thousand times.

One-sixteenth of the times it would take to fill Taylor Field in Regina.

One time they played it backward & Jack Ruby pulled a bullet out of Lee Harvey Oswald & Lee Harvey quit grimacing & so on & you know it continued so that there was Jack Kennedy's head all in one piece & the Americans leaving Cuba & that is how American history happens on television.

But in Canada history consists of writing

history. For that reason history is filled with mistakes & most of them are written by poetry. The novel can only sit back & try to understand.

Beavers cant even read. They use old book pages to wrap their naked bodies against the wintery blast off Lake Superior.

George Bowering is still sitting at his desk & now he is scratching out line after line. Thus a little bit of history disappears.

When a brick falls out of the Citadel it makes no difference.

When they try to rebuild Fort Dream with epoxy glue it is a vain effort.

But when George Bowering decides to scratch out history he would be making history if history wasnt making history.

But he knew. The novel was putting on the old fatigues & going to war again.

PART FOUR:
The Black Mountain Influence

Chapter XXXI

If I want this to be a post-modern novel I'd better forget about history.

You'll forget about history if you just quit writing it for reasons outlined above & by & by history will forget about you.

You can take my word for it.

I promist you a novel & I would like to keep my word but if I keep my word you cant take my word for it & most of all I want to be a man who stands by his word & how are we going to handle all that.

Maybe I should carve this novel in a rock face next to Lake Superior. Then we wouldnt be able to do number one & number two but we could do number three.

Number three is standing by your word.

Number one was waking up.

You could look it up.

You know me, Al.

You know Al, he was standing by someone's word on a rock face next to Lake Superior.
He was swearing under his breath.

I thought this was going to be about war & now it is about words. A piece about words. One of them was there in the beginning & it was number one.
It is about & I hate it when the writer says this is about & it is now about that too, it is though about our words you will notice & their words you will notice if you're a little sharper, especially if you are one of them but that's the publisher's concern.
The publisher is my regular publisher.
A Canadian.

The Canadian publisher lookt at the sentence & said is Bowering hedging, why didnt he name the publisher.

Wow, is this ever a post-modern novel.
Frank, is this a post-modern novel.
I'm sorry if you werent expecting a post-modern novel.
I wasnt expecting any of it.
That's what I mean.

If you are expecting a post-modern novel it isnt a post-modern novel.
So I'm not sorry after all.
Unless you were expecting a post-modern

novel.

You might wind up with a short sad book.

You should wind up with a world I never made.
That's an obscure paradox I dont want to deal with.

I'll let that egg hatch.

I'll let it be till laid.

Al stood by those words & wondered how to translate them into a poem. It would be a post-ancient poem.

He found out he couldnt translate them because he was there now & it was much later.

He translated himself & the poem was transcribed on an old tree from a nearby hill.

Chapter XXXII

Let me tell you a story. It is all about American literature & Canadian literature. What we share is the Great Lakes & the Pacific Ocean & that other one the Atlantic Ocean. Where Atlantis is, under.

Al stood by Lake Superior & lookt out at it. Airplanes flew over it every day & all the passengers were imprest. They couldnt see anything but water. No they couldnt & neither could I. Something is trying to stop my hand. It's Al.
He is standing by the superior lake & musing. This is what he muses. That is these are the words his muse offers him, he being a post-ancient poet.

That in American literature they are all above the water or on the water. Chasing the great white whale or two years before the mast, & in Canadian literature they are in the water or underwater. That is why we keep claiming Malcolm Lowry is

Canadian literature, because he wrote a book called Ultramarine & I keep thinking of Submarine.

American literature is above the ground or on the top of the water dont shoot till you see the whites of their eyes. Canadian literature, well Canadian literature. One is walking into the lake & becoming an ancient fish, one is hitting an iceberg & going down, one is looking for her father's words on a rock face under the surface, it was a Canadian publisher, business as usual. Another was slipping below the waves at Cape Flattery.

I said American literature was also on top of the ground, but Canadian literature is under the ground not underground but under the ground, under the ground or under the snow or under the ice. What are we doing under here.

Al was musing about this & wondering if he should go for a swim. He went for a swim in Cuba one time & he thought about his grandfather digging into the ground.

At war with the U.S. we have to dig in, but what do we do. We hide under the ground.

This is getting political in a funny way.

I will teach you my townspeople how to perform a funeral for you have it over a troupe of artists unless you scour the earth you have the ground sense necessary.

Al hated black, mountainous poetry because it

was on the high ground.

He resolved not to go swimming.

Tom Thompson's body came to the surface.

This is what his muse said.

Better to make it with a tree than freeze your balls off under a cold lake.

He had been up here for three days & he hadnt yet caught a glimpse of a beaver.

He saw a man walking westward with a slim volume of waterlogged poetry & a maple leaf stuck to the back of his sweater.

Tom Thompson's body floated ashore & bobbed against the rock face, obliterating the ancient poem.

The old words were gone, but to the west Al could see that the sweater would hold the maple leaf forever.

Chapter XXXIII

In their literature they always shoot the whites out of their eyes. But we dont have eyes, we have pearls that were our eyes, underwater.

The geographical history of Ontario proves it.

Al the Canadian knew all there was to know about the geographical history of Ontario. They say the 401 Highway runs east & west. That is not geography that is history. He wrote it so it was history. Almost caught myself there.

In Ontario they have counties, they used to have counties because in England they had counties but now they have counties because the U.S. has counties. Ask the Canadian nationalist professor from Ottawa name of Sparrow, he's paid by the CIA to give Canadian nationalism a bad name.

Al the real Canadian reads Nineteenth Century maps of the Ontario counties. They are full of family names. Evangeline isnt there at all. Her name is written on a rock face in Louisiana. Americans stand by their words, right there.

If you try to stand by their words they'll shoot the whites out of your eyes.

In the War of 1812 Canada lost the Great Lakes campaign because we had no submarines.

You wont find that in Canadian literature.

In Canadian literature you'll find Mrs O'Leary leading her cow thru the geography of an Ontario county to warn General Brock the Americans are coming with guns in their hands.

Won if by land. Lost if by sea.

Where the fuck are the submarines, said the eloquent General Brock.

They named a university library after him & filled it with Canadian literature.

This is not Canadian literature I'm writing. I'm making post-modern Canadian history.

Ask Al. Ask Frank.

Ask the name of the lion.

That's what Al did in Stanley Park, when he was writing the geographical history of Canada.

You could look it up.

Sparrow said we got to stop them Americans from getting the beautiful Okanagan Valley but he wrote it the way the Americans do in Washington, Okanogan, with an O.

It was a dead give away. He went to college in

the U.S. That's where he was recruited by the CIA. He was also approacht by the NKVD. He copied the spelling of the OK Valley from their instructions I mean the CIA. That was AOK with them. Back in B.C. we are careful about our letters.

There's a lot of Canadian literature at the bottom of Lake Okanagan.

Al the Canadian tied some rocks to Tom Thompson's body. They had broken off the rock face. Now he mused as Tom's body sank in twenty feet of water.

This is becoming a mystery novel.

Who killed Tom Thompson.

Chapter XXXIV

Every time less than the pulsation of the artery is equal in its period & value to six thousand years.

I like literature I mean prose that is cut into short sections. I will read more pages of literature that is cut into short sections before I turn out the light than literature in long sections like Samuel Beckett.

Six thousand years. That is how long the words were on the wall before he read them. It was just like yesterday. It was less than a second ago. The ghost of the writer was standing by his words. This too was a ghost-written novel. The Indians, well the Indians too had a literature. We wrote it for them. Up here in heaven.
Do you know what ghost-written means?
In Canadian it is the same as hag-ridden.
Ask Peggy & Brian.

The death of the novel was a Canadian mystery.

Al the detective drove his car further west, thinking of clues. What did he have? A body in the lake & some words on the rock face. Not much to go on.

If he didnt have much to go on what about me.

I cant give him another clue. Not until whoever is writing me gives me another clue.

Maybe an overturned Quaker Oats box.

That's it, said Al, & pulled over outside Dryden to jot some words in his spiral notebook made of fibres désencrées et recyclées.

He was right about where I first saw a moose.

The pieces were beginning to come together.

He had a victim. All he was missing was a motive, & a suspect.

You know me, Al.

The victim meanwhile was lying on the bottom of Lake Superior, next to a Seventeenth Century ship filled with animal skins. This was Tom Thompson.

My eyes shifted from there to Dryden. I am the author. At the best of times I am not. When I am the author is when I am the suspect. Some days it doesnt pay to get out of bed. Under the snow of northern Ontario.

Al drove off the highway into Dryden. The air

was filled with the smell of recycled trees. He made a phone call from a box on the main drag. Next to the box was a shopping cart. It was empty. A few moments earlier it had been filled with Canadian literature. The sparrow's fall.

Oh no, that's too complicated altogether.

Now I'm not the author again.

A few minutes later Al the detective was tooling his red Ford Galaxie toward Kenora. He was smiling thru a four-cent cigar. He was wearing sunglasses, a white shirt with the sleeves rolled up, nondescript unprest blue slacks & nondescript black oxfords.

He was smiling because he knew the Canadian mystery would be solved in the west.

Chapter XXXV

Written language should not be led she said only converstion should be led it is what is said & she was right again even as I write again.

Now there is a book I have been reading for nine months & I'm not finisht yet, not yet, nearly but not yet & yet not nearly.

You see what I mean. If you've been following you've been led, but it hasnt.

Now David McFadden has already written to command, isnt that a lovely word it closes & then it opens, command!, David McFadden closes up at the ends, but he has written to command me to change the name of this novel.

He wants me to call it The Black Mountain Influence.

But I've got the Al the private eye speeding west in a car full of burglar tools.

See this section is full of titles & near titles. Some more of that fancy dancing Angela was complaining about but if you identify with Al the private eye you can figure it out. You can figure it out.

I've got Al speeding west with a car full of private eye equipment so I think I'll call it The Black Mountain Mystery.

To us out here it is a mystery but to them back east or in a text book it is the Black Mountain puzzle.

Once a woman who has made herself famous writing about Canadian literature askt me whereabouts in Vancouver is Black Mountain.

I told her it was across Burrard Inlet on the north shore or just beyond.

Just recently I found out that was true after all. I think.

That's how the Black Mountain Influence works.

Sometimes when people ask me about the Black Mountain Influence I tell them the closest I ever got was Montenegro.

I had two Yugoslavian friends when I was in high school.

I went to Montenegro in 1966 & lookt across the mountains at Albania. Albania is a mystery to me.

Frank Mahovlich is a Yugoslavian from back east & now he's in a text book, or some day he will be if my reputation grows. Frank Mahovlich is my travel agent. If I'm reading this to you right now Frank Mahovlich arranged my airplane ticket to get here as long as you are not in Vancouver or even the North Shore.

Speaking of hockey which I always happened to imagine on the radio from Watrous there is also Eddie Shore. It's on the edge of Eddie Lake.

You'll notice this novel is full of lakes just like Canada.

Al the private eye noticed this too, just as he was driving by Lake Louise.

That's how long it took to write this chapter.

Chapter XXXVI

Feeling the familiar & unnameable urge, he put aside his work & engaged the poem or rather the novel again. This was the mystery. Not the puzzle of the post-modern, but the ancient mystery, he felt almost as if he would find himself at the end of the sentence at last. At first he did & then in the middle it was composition & once again he was happy that it wasnt the last. It would last.

Thirty-six, imagine that, thirty-six. Why, he remembered thirty-six. It was just like yesterday.

Al the private dick was finally there.

Black Mountain.

At the top he was exhausted but he had a perfect view of the city. It was the jewel of the Pacific. He made a note of that.

He lookt north & saw that scenery had no beginning middle or end.

He lookt closer & saw a Douglas Fir. Looking thru his private eyeglasses he could make out a heart carved in the skin. The words inside the heart said Evangeline & Mac.

He remembered from The 42nd Parallel that Mac had ridden the rails to Vancouver, but he didnt remember a girl with that name, & he didnt remember Mac climbing Black Mountain. Or any mountain. But the novel was called USA, & that was enough for Al. He had pinned down the Black Mountain Influence.

Some years earlier Al had ridden the rails to Vancouver. Literary figures were always doing that.

The best your author ever did was to ride on top of a boxcar from Lawrence to Testalinda.

Al lookt at the Black Mountian Influence for a while. If he had been looking south he would have seen the Fraser River effluence. The Spaniards had called it the White River. Al would have liked that. He saw as much as possible in black & white.

This world was made a few moments ago, & what we call the past is our memories creating history.

Canadian history is writing history. We have begun doing that very recently. Within the past few moments.

Al took the chair lift back down to the North Shore, but first he took a moment to plant something that would grow into a mighty oak. He had brought it all the way from that other Nart Shar, where they fly a flag with little oaks on it.

He said there that ought to offset the Black Mountain Influence.

He felt a little like the carpenter of Galilee coming down off the Mount of Olives.

He was trying to make a beginning for a new scenery. This happened moments ago.

Chapter XXXVII

What are you doing on this mountain said the guard, this is Black Mountain & it has been sold to the University of Calgary Library. Holus bolus.

I dont feel like arguing, said Al the gumshoe.

I was watching all the time from behind a Douglas Fir. Now I stept out & showed myself.

I dont feel like writing, I said.

I thought I would leave the rest of the page blank. I got a new pen instead. Really. You could have seen it if you were here. This is Canadian literature. It all happened a moment ago.

Another moment ago.

The detective disappeared. The moment I stopt writing about him.

The mighty oak never grew on that mountain.

This all sounds like a bunch of endings.

Will Canadian literature have a beginning

middle & end? Will the University of Calgary Library buy up all the scenery in the country & put it on reserve for English 429?

Of course any one who writes anything is talking to herself. Ordinarily anyone finishes anything. But not in writing.

I can make the detective appear anytime I want to. See, here he is. That is the real Black Mountain Influence.

& who is doing the same thing with me right now, & listen, if right now is fifty years from now when I'm lying at the bottom of Lake Superior remember it happened moments ago.

The chief joy of this is that the language is so sensible. So clear & so sensible. Even Al the gumshoe would be able to follow it. Even the Sparrow would be able to see the good Presbyterian Canadian sense in it, but he would spell Canadian with an O.

Even Brian would take his writing implement out of the O in the Douglas Fir long enough to say that's right, I never saw it so clearly before.

Coming up out of the depths of Lake Baskatong, Peggy would say George I knew it all along, you love this country.

It's in speaking that ideas come to us, words, & then we, in our own words, we find perhaps everything, the city too, the garden, & then we are orphans no longer.

The words will make a world.

All the time I am writing this Canadian book I am not writing something else & it is the invisible book I am not writing. There is one of those for every book that is written.

We have just solved the great Canadian problem of the one-book novelist.

That's why we need detectives like Al, to track down all that invisible Canadian literature.

Chapter XXXVIII

I certainly do know what Al the investigator is going to do next. He is going to smoke a cigar.

I smoke a cigar & I tried to write I spoke a cigar, I smoke a cigar every time I write a chapter. This is the thirty-eighth cigar for this book. Light up a cigar & read it. You will be getting your mouth around Canadian literature. That is more than they manage to do on de Maisonneuve Boulevard in Montreal.

Al went to the wrong hotel beer parlour on Granville Street & smoked a cigar. It was a Trump cigar & it cost a nickle. It was clencht between his front teeth & the end was all wet & chewed up.

The cigar means more to Canadian literature than the beaver.

A.J.M. Smith smokes Reo cigars out of silver coloured tubes.

David McFadden smokes Budgie cigars when they come on special.

The cigar means more to Canadian literature than the Black Mountain Influence.

Joe Rosenblatt, well Joe Rosenblatt. He smokes straight dark cigars from Spadina Avenue.

I'm the only poet under the Black Mountain Influence who smokes cigars in Canada. I learned to smoke cigars in London Ontario, on Dundas Street.

Milton Acorn smokes cigars made in Cuba. They are very expensive. He has a lot of taste. He has tasted his cigar.

I dont think Peggy had a chapter on cigars in her book. She made a big mistake because she doesnt smoke anything.

I feel as if I wont survive many more cigars.

Andrew Suknaski puts poems inside the silver tubes from Reo cigars & floats them down the South Saskatchewan River. The last time I saw him was in Cole's book store on Yonge Street.

A few chapters ago it was trees & now it is streets, isnt that interesting.

Graeme Gibson smokes El Productos. They come five to a package, there's another literary in-joke.

Cigars mean more to Canadian literature than snow.

Smoking cigars is modern but smoking marijuana is post-modern. So post-modern is old hat. Put that in your pipe & smoke it.

Al sat in the beer parlour smoking a second cigar, & put together the pieces. He now knew that Tom Thompson had not been killed by the Black Mountain Influence.

He remembered that several chapters ago it was lakes. The Black Mountain Influence wasnt interested in lakes. Raymond Knister was interested in lakes. Peggy was interested in lakes. A.J.M. Smith was interested in lakes.

It had to be the lakes.

They were surrounded by Canadian geography & Canadian literature, & the Group of Seven.

Al collected his change off the table, leaving only the nickles with Monticellos on them. Each one represented a cigar he wouldnt smoke.

He would have to follow the mystery to Kleinburg, Ontario.

Chapter XXXIX

"If you can hear it you have the right to speak."

& that's the trouble with Canadian literature. Canadian literature was once written by fake Hurons & now it is written by the Immigrant Experience. It is never written by the Black Mountain Influence. It is written by anthropologists who know what a maple leaf looks like but dont know how it speaks.

In a masterpiece there is no thought. No thought about. There is no thought about. Just in Canadian literature. That is the trouble with Canadian literature.

Canadian literature is always right. That is the trouble with Canadian literature.

This is not Canadian literature.

I love this country I write.

This is a novel made of the sound of leaves turning. It is not Canadian literature.

If you are right you may be only Canadian literature. But that is not the right to speak.
Canadian literature will never understand this.
Canadian literature will not understand this novel.

Is this writing or is this thinking.
You cant hear it if you are already thinking.
Whatever else poetry is not freedom. No it is not. Poetry is not freedom. The truth will make you free but poetry will not.

Tom Thompson was free. Al the sleuth was not a religious man but he understood this. Tom Thompson was free but his paintings were not. They were hanging in the Bank of Commerce.
The Imperial Bank of Commerce.

Louis Riel was free but his people were not. Louis Riel died with a T in his hand. It stood for the Toronto Dominion Bank. His people owe a lot of money to the TD bank.
Evangeline was free but her poem wasnt. Her poem was in a safety deposit box in the Bank of Nova Scotia.

Canadian literature is a lot like a bank. It has Group of Seven paintings all over the wall & it is always all lockt up at night.
I'm sure my wife likes this one, it is not

obscure at all. We have just experienced a grand simile.

Al the bloodhound just loved a simile. He felt at home there. He felt as if he had both feet firmly placed on the ground. Good flat ground. Like a patient table, waiting to be etherized.

Sorry, there I go again.

Tom Thompson was free from similies. He had neither foot on the ground. The canoe tipt over & he fell from Canadian literature right into the lake. This was the Northern Experience.

Canadian literature righted itself & proceeded to float with the current. It was emptied of the human form, just like a Group of Seven painting.

It closed at three p.m. & opened again the next morning at ten.

Chapter XL

Now I want to leave off Canadian literature but I want to say this.

It is so easy to write something & make it appear as if it is there. We all like to read about something as if it is there. This is not writing it is thinking, I mean this, yes a mirror on the floor.

It is all around us, writing that makes it appear as if it is there. That is writing about or writing of or what is it it is writing as if it is there. The reader loves Canadian literature because he can just about see it it is as if it is there.

But if you hear it you have the right to speak.

In the best writing it is there.

In the best writing it is there & now it is not it it is writing.

If you are lucky you are reading writing.

Put it another way, it is not a clear lake with a body on the bottom.

It is a body & who needs a lake.

This is the real body of literature.

This is not a mystery & it is not a puzzle, it is certainly not a puzzle.

You are not reading a murder mystery. If you want to know the truth Tom Thompson fell in the lake. He lay in repose just this side of the world's longest undefended border.

Now I want to leave off Canadian literature so I will despatch Al the private eye. It gets so tiresome to see a private eye become everybody's eye piece.

Or everybody's mouth piece.

Let me tell you you can round up every Ontario high school teacher in the Central Canada Experience & you will still never do it.

You can drown every poet from Antigonish to the Queen Charlotte Islands & you will never do it. You can write the Canadian Literary History & try to make it seem to be there right in front of a couple thousand private eyes & you'll never do it. You'll never do it because Canadian Literary History is writing Canadian Literary History, kapeesh?

If you think this is an essay in Canadian Literary History you are wrong, or you are right, but if you are right too bad for you because if you are right you are only in Canadian literature you arent hearing it.

Whatever it, is.

Stan sat on the wharf on Ward's Island, staring into the slightly stained water of Lake Ontario. He saw a book lying on the bottom, its pages riffling in the current. He reacht down his arm's length & retrieved it.

It was the Tercentenary History of Canada, Volume III, From Laurier to King, MCMVIV—MCMXLV.

Stan was a semi-Canadian publisher. Half of him threw the book a hundred feet out into the lake. The other half brought it back to the office & kept it in a tropical fish tank.

PART FIVE:
The Pretty Good Canadian Novel

Chapter XLI

Well was that the end yes & no. It was the end of the mystery & the end of the decade & the end of the Black Mountain Influence & the end of the geographical mystery of Canadian literature & it was in a way the end of Canadian literature.

Who killed Tom Thompson. I couldnt say who killed Cock Robin. You see this is not a children's novel but there is a rime already.

Well there is a rime already.

This is a serial novel.

Ask Stan.

Stan came from Edmonton. He came from Edmonton & arrived in Toronto on the bus. He was sitting there with an old ordinary Doukhobor hat on his head, a paper shopping bag between his feet, he never said a word on the bus. He wasnt much of a man for words. He was in love with

139

books. He didnt read them. He loved them.

Isnt this a surprise, I had no idea I was going to tell you about Stan. He just arrived & this is not the 42nd parallel it is the 41st discretion.

Writing is not parallel it is serial.

Stan, well what do we know about Stan. I saw him the second time Mr Gold got him high. He was standing against the wall behind Pierre Berton. Pierre Berton is from further north & west than Edmonton. Stan was standing against the wall & he didnt have a word to say.

The last time I saw Stan he was not printing words he was pressing numbers on a small electronic box. Words are for a printer & numbers are for a publisher.

He always smiles.

The small electronic box works in series. It is a serial box. That is how literature works, I mean that, not seeming to put that in front of your eyes but putting this next to your ear.

It's in speaking that ideas come to us.

The perfect type of the strong silent man is the suicide.

Am I saying that Stan is silent. No I am saying that he is not much of a man for words.

There is a strong possibility that he will print these words.

You would be surprised how often publishers

get into novels.

At Stan's place the novelists get into the publishing business. This is not Canadian literature. It is mindless beaver freaks. The beaver is not a national emblem it is a union label.

Ask Stan.

Ask him why he has a printing press & a beaver on his books while the Nationalists have a foreign spider on their books & an alien owner & postgraduate degrees from across the line.

Forgive this ranting. It is the middle of the novel, where all the axes are ground. It is the ground work.

Chapter XLII

It is the ground sense necessary.

We all grow out of the ground & that is the way we grow. I grew out of obdurate ground in the Okanagan Valley, stones & sand, & when I go back to the desert I feel called on to pronounce it beautiful.

& if you say this isnt the way a novel is supposed to grow what can I say. What the hell, am I supposed to decide what Stan did next.

If you expect me to do that well why dont you follow me around for a day & make me be continuous. I'll put a few dishes in the dishwasher & you say a job worth doing is a job worth doing well.

Well I see Stan once in a while maybe once a year & we exchange a few words. He has never come off second in the deal.

He has both his feet on the ground.

None of his authors has ever drowned.

Where he grew up there are rivers & lakes & ponds & creeks & he never once fell victim to any of them.

A lot of water has gone over the dam since then. Take one look at him & you know the ground he grew out of. Alberta, & not southern Alberta where the ones who all look the same live. This all happened a few minutes ago. Standing in a doorway in Toronto you recognize this in an instant.

You will notice I'm not ranting about them & us now. This is a philosophical novel, where all is considered, reasoned, balanced & here goes number four again. I always used to list three & now I list four. I am in my forties & so is this book. We breathe together.

This is the conspiratorial view of history.

Canadian history is conspiring to write history.

When he was a baby in Alberta he knew nothing, people poked him & dandled him & cooed at him & askt them what his name was & he was a baby named Stan.

Isnt that funny. A baby named Stan.

This is a short sad book but it has funny stuff in it. A baby named Stan is as funny as the great Canadian sonnet.

Here you have a five star important message

about post-modern publishing.

Even a three-year-old kid named Stan is pretty funny. Even in Alberta where a lot of things that are funny arent thought to be funny.
They would try to get the queen to wear a white cowboy hat in Alberta.

Stan came out of Alberta wearing a black Doukhobor hat.
Pretty soon all the Toronto hippies were wearing black Doukhobor hats.
Al the detective never wore a hat. He wore a twenty-year-old necktie with a five-year-old knot in it.
He thought everything Stan printed was a hoax. He thought it grew in foreign ground. He was a suspicious detective & not much of a detective.

Chapter XLIII

Now you dont have a novel unless you have a person & then you have a person talking to another person & later on perhaps many people but usually a person talking to another person.

Stan is running water in the bathtub, & in comes Carol wearing nothing but some beads around her waist. Why do we say Stan, because we have been talking about Stan, & that's the way it goes, the novel.

It could have been Laurier Lapierre. They were in the back of the crowd that was watching Carol having a bath & Stan began talking with Laurier Lapierre. He said you are very British Laurier because you are wearing a shirt & tie & two sweaters & a waistcoat & a jacket. Are you wearing long underwear.

Yes I am, said Laurier.

& you keep cool, dont you.

Yes I do, said Laurier. Does that really mean I am British.

Stan gestured to a person nearby, with sandy thick hair & a sweater under his jacket. See him? You're English arent you, he askt the man. Yes I am said the Englishman. So you see said Stan.

Laurier lookt proud. He tried to make an English moue.

You should get a bunch of sports car suits said Stan, & some white shoes.

Going out the door Laurier was holding a walking stick. He gestured to his shoe lifted up behind him. It was a white sandal.

That's not right thought Stan, but he was surprised.

Oh did you want to take a bath too, he said to Carol. For a man with little time for words he was talking a lot so maybe it wasnt Stan maybe it was me. I can do anything I want with people in a novel, & then the publisher can decide what to do with it.

On television Jack McClelland askt me when I was going to write another novel for him.

How about a short sad book I askt him.

He didnt seem to like that idea.

It was just an idea.

I cant do anything I want anyway. What I want

to do is write a novel in which I will not be able to write what I want.

A ghost-ridden novel.

Stan didnt want to take a bath. He was running the water because he had taken a long happy piss in the tub & it wasnt draining well though there were two holes, one at the end & one at the middle. He had heard Carol telling Vic that she was thinking of having a bath & he thought the door was lockt & it really was me you know & the pee went on a lot longer than I expected & it wasnt all that happy for that reason it was filled with anxiety.

I'll wait for both of you said Stan, he was relieved to see that it lookt as if nothing was in the tub but some clear tap water.

On the door it said The Family of Vic D'Or. This was the peopling of the landscape, a typical pun inside the coach house.

Chapter XLIV

You want to write about the country you love & this is where you have to start, with one person & the other person. The whole world is that way & so is a novel. In Canada the novel is not writing the novel, two people are, all the time.

That is why Laurier Lapierre is always interviewing someone & why he is truly bicultural & why he is in the novel or on CBC. Two Solitudes was all wrong. Two solitudes may be very modern but they will not make a novel.

Laurier Lapierre was interviewing John A. Macdonald on CBC. He askt him about the National Policy.

We have to keep the CPR out of Montana & get Evangeline back from Louisiana, said Big Mac.

Now that's not bicultural.

Not even with Black Diamond Cheese.

Nibbling on Black Diamond Cheese, Stan listened to the novel on the radio. He was adding up figures that told the true story of Canadian publishing.

If they dont want to read Canadian novels, you cant stop them said one of the girls in the office. She was wearing a tee shirt with a picture of Laurier Lapierre on it. Her name was Marie-Ange.

Isnt that a Scottish name, askt Stan.

You fool, you poule, she said.

Her full flow of talk was assuming obsessive proportions, it seemed to me.

Naturally Marie-Ange, far from stupid, senst this, & putting down the Ferré disc she went out of the press room more quickly, if anything, than she'd entered. You're a cold fish, I told myself. You might have been nicer. Must be the change in the weather.

It was raining nickles again.

The huge chimney stack in Sudbury was malfunctioning, spewing currency all over Northern Ontario & as far south as Rochester, New York. There a second-generation American named Gabe Dumont pickt up a coin & turned it over.

First time I ever saw a beaver, he said aloud.

When was the first time you ever saw a beaver, Laurier was asking John. They had settled into a kind of familiarity bestowed by the soundproof studio. On radio the public could not see John's bottle of Mortlach single malt.

To tell you the truth I've never seen one, Lory, said the P.M.

Well, while we're making confessions, I can tell you that I've never seen them pouring hot maple syrup on the snow, said Laurier Lapierre, cool as a cucumber in his two sweaters & jacket. Even under colour lamps on TV he never broke into a sweat.

You know, Lory, I think that maple syrup business is just in text books, or back east, said the P.M.

Stan wasnt listening any more. He was following Marie-Ange's footsteps in the snow of the back alley behind Huron Street.

He didnt know why he was following her but she was as sweet as maple sugar pie & he was a publisher in pursuit of the Pretty Good Canadian Novel.

Chapter XLV

Am I supposed to decide what Stan did next. Is Stan supposed to decide what he did next. I insist, I still insist that this is not Canadian literature written by somebody with a Scottish name. In the U.S.A. there arent many Scottish names. In Canadian literature there are almost nothing but Scottish names. This is a northern country, that is the latest line in Canadian literature.

Stan followed her footprints thru the snow, you see the chapters develop from one to the next, & here is the snow again, I sit here coldly composing the text. Consciousness is how it is composed.

He followed her footprints all night. They were headed east. Toward the text books.

In the morning he found himself in front of David's house.

David opened his eyes. April air pluckt at the curtains like breath behind a veil. It held a hint of real warmth to come, but the linen chill of the night still sharpened it. Clean limb shadows palpitated with precision & immaculacy on the breathing ground outside. The whole morning glistened fresh as the flesh of an alder sapling when the bark was first peeled from it to make a whistle. It glinted bright as the split rock-maple, flashing for a minute in the sun as it was tost onto the woodpile.

Jesus, I feel shitty in the morning, thought David. All this description & sentimentality feels like a bloody screech hangover.

He went to the window to see what it really lookt like. There was Stan, who had just made some limited edition prints in the fresh brown snow.

What you looking for, Stan, he said, his mind fighting to put down a simile about light sparkling off a flounder newly pulled out of the morning Atlantic.

Have you see the Pretty Good Canadian Novel, askt Stan.

Funny, they were just talking about that on the CBC, remarkt David, all the time watching the ground breathing the first breaths of a promise thru the mantle of morning whiteness.

Who was, said Stan, nearly asleep with exhaustion. I should have worn snow shoes, he thought.

A couple of guys with Scottish names, said

David.

I shouldnt have found myself in front of David's house, Stan thought.

He did.

The whole morning glistened like the brilliance of an RCMP flashlight on the teeth of Tom Thompson's corpse.

It did.

What were they talking about, askt Stan, trying to be polite & thinking too that any time now David would be buckling on some snow shoes & striding purposively & lonely over the carpet of new snow. He was that sort of boy.

They mentioned shooting a pig with a .22, shooting a calf with a '30-.30, following a girl thru the streets.

Oh, the great Canadian culture hunt, said Stan.

As he walkt off eastward, David shouted after him, I hope you find her. There followed a series of similies, but Stan was out of earshot.

Chapter XLVI

Novels always have the emotion of the novelist in them. Thick heart felt emotion. The blood of others pumpt by the man in the attic.

& people say why are you doing archaic avant-garde writing. This is warmed over Gertrude Stein there I said her name why are you doing it.

They mean I'm not allowed to do it.

If I do it it is an accident & if I do it it is right because she was looking for how the mind works & if she found out I can find out accidentally, I have a mind.

The spirit is willing.

It is a ghost-written novel but it is not the ghost of Miss Stein it is the ghost of the novel. Alive & kicking.

So I'll watch, nasty me, you kicking whores pass. Remember that's a slit thru the romantic.

Stan the man we were following was cold on the trail that spring of the Pretty Good Canadian Novel. He followed her bilingual heart down the St Lawrence River where Canadian history happened in the text books.

Spring leapt quickly into full summer that year. One day people woke & saw that the buds had become leaves & the mud dried into friable earth. There was great activity over all the parish as the planting was completed. Before it was finisht the first blackflies appeared in the spruce of the distant forest; then they were in the maple grove on the ridge behind the Tallard land. By the Queen's birthday or May twenty-fourth it was almost as hot as mid-summer. The heat simmered in delicate gossamers along the surface of the plain, cloud formations built themselves up thru the mornings, & by afternoon they were majestic above the river. The first green shoots of the seeds that had been consecrated on Saint Marc's Day appeared above the soil in the sunshine. Quebec was really being described.

Stan askt everyone he saw whether they had seen the Pretty Good Canadian Novel heading this way. Nobody could understand a word he said.

"Imaginieres frontières de la transparence," they shouted.

"Je suis un fils déchu de race surhumaine," they cried.

What, said Stan, his Alberta Doukhobor hat shading his eyes. What.

"Je n'ai pas de nom, anonyme, je suis anonyme," they snarled, waving their crude hoes & rakes as they stood in the rocky soil where the consecrated shoots made spots of green under the majestic clouds.

The clouds were brown, & composed chiefly of iron sulphide.

I've publisht Nicole Brossard, yelled Stan, I've publisht Victor-Lévy Beaulieu.

Never heard of them, they replied. Try a little further down the mighty river, at the Paris of North America.

The place was full of novelists, he thought, but half of them were Jewish, maybe he would find Marie-Ange among the other half. Or maybe she was Marie-Ange-Rachel now.

Chapter XLVII

The day before yesterday I'm interrupting now or it is, but then sometimes discontinuity is really an older & wiser continuity & then you will likely say maybe not out loud well look at this continuity who ever would have thought. Who ever would have thought it.

Well as I started to say the day before yesterday I finally & certainly did see a beaver. Not to mention oh really? yesterday I mused upon how people were probably saying maybe even saying out loud, to a friend or wife of the reader, that is not how you spell Tom Thomson.

Well it wasnt Tom Thomson it was Tom Thompson. Just as earlier it wasnt Van Horne it was Crump. He is a policeman in a play by Eric (bp) Nickle. That is, under the weather.

I was with my daughter & the beaver was behind two layers of fine mesh steel. It can bite your finger right off. I told her. Even if you wrap yourself in the flag like Three Fingers Brown & Ed Delahanty. Delsing gets baseball in whenever he can.

The beaver stood with his front paws on the mesh & lookt at us, he was all wet & muddy after all a beaver is an underwater animal, thus a candidate for Canadian literature.

The beaver stood with his four fingers, no Walt Disney critter he, on the mesh & lookt at us, & he moaned. I bent over to hear, I didnt know whether to believe my ears but neither do you though I have to because this novel does not always speak to me with a stentorian voice. & every time I bent over the beaver moaned. Now I didnt know about that.

What about all you people from Ontario did you know that.

I just found out about the policeman today. There you are, the day before yesterday yesterday & today. It all happened in the last minute or so. Half a cigar ago.

"*A Short Sad Book* is a fast-moving, entertaining & bawdy novel." —Washington *Star.*

Stan was nearing le Grand Maury Awl now, following the tracks of the Pretty Good Canadian Novel to the edge of a Goyish lake. He was excited by the Canadianness of it all. He heard a beaver's tail slap the surface of the still water. A loon's cry rang out. He was tempted to construct a quick Canadian documentary fiction.

Let them think I've drowned, he thought. It would serve them right. He had seen a drowned woman once at Shawbridge, & the thought of his own face bloated like that—Irwin hanging for it, the bastard, & his father maybe feeling sorry he hadnt treated him as well as Lennie—made a hot lump in . . . .

Then he remembered Marie-Rachel. That's probably exactly what she did, he thought.

That bitch.

He knew just where she was.

Under the black shadow of the Mount Royal Influence, among the discarded crutches.

Chapter XLVIII

Stan was in le Grand Maury All, & now you see there is no interruption. Purdon Clarke said he hated unrest & that was the trouble with the Modern & now James Dickey says he hates discontinuity & that is the trouble with the post-modern, it doesnt have any capital letters.

Stan was actually in Montreal, he had followed the trail of the PGCN all the way to Brother André's heart.

There you are, an acute & an apostrophe. When was the last time you saw them together. I told you this was a truly to use Greg Curnoé's word bicultural event. Victor-Lévy Beaulieu is my brother, Andrew.

He imagined that Marie-Rachel had a babushka on her head & was kneeling in front of Brother André's heart, wanting acutely to possess the spirit that was beating there. She had beaten Stan there by less than an hour, after wasting all that time with the flashy Jewish kid at the lake.

Since the heart had been stolen you couldnt see it anymore but if you had faith you knew it was there & if you didnt have faith what were you doing there in the first place.

She would always want to come back & visit for a day in the middle of the winter.

& now you understand, you have heard this story before. The novelist has only at the most two ideas in a lifetime & he plays out the variations before your eyes.

The smart ones here recognized Marie-Evangeline.

In the sky over the mountain a faint pink streak appeared. The rim of trees was a dark fringe against the pink light. On the mountain slopes the great homes & massive apartments were still in the grey shadow. As sunlight to the east glinted on the canal & toucht church spires & towers, the city began to stir with a faint low hum.

Hmmmmmmmm. Hrrrrrrr.

The really smart ones will remember that

Peggy has been around since Chapter VI & now here she is & here is Jim & Jim would like her name to be McAlpine. Around the mountain. So it goes.

That was a post-modern tag.

You're it.

Stan the man waited among the discarded trusses & fought back sleep. He felt as if he was getting unerringly close to the Pretty Good you know what.

When Marie-Marion came back down the stairs she showed no surprise.

Why does your name keep changing, askt Stan, but this was not the question he had walkt three hundred & fifty miles to put to her or to the Frye school in General.

When I was born in Dundas, Ontario, she replied, they called me Castor Canadiensis. I always thought that was a dirty trick.

She disappeared before his eyes.

It was as if he had never seen her.

The edible beaver. His curiosity had turned to love, & now he had lost her again.

Chapter XLIX

I think it is obvious, I love this country. Once I got a grant to spend two years in England but I went to London Ontario instead. Another time I got a grant to spend a year in Austria but I went to Vancouver, British Columbia instead. That was a good thing. Those are the only two places where I ever had a house. When I got to London Ontario & when I got to Vancouver I yankt out the stakes that were holding up the peonies, this is true. I pulled up stakes & stayed. In England they believe in stakes to hold up the peonies but I dont.

That is why Stan is moving around so much. On top of the mountain he found a stake a poet had driven into the snow the previous winter. He pulled it out & threw it off the mountain. The mountain wasnt alpine & the stake was only modern. He found out where the oak seeds had been planted & dug them up.

He was not looking for poetry he was in pursuit of the Pretty Good Canadian Novel, there wasnt much time left, he would settle for the Pretty Good Canadian Novella but he wouldnt settle.

Not Stan.

He wouldnt take that lying down.

You get my point?

Try driving that into the Canadian Shield.

He had arrived on the very tick of two. She had been there twenty minutes earlier, very hot, but pale from excitement & fatigue; she had jogged—sometimes breaking into a run—for nearly half of a mile, lugging the heavy portmanteau. She had been in a state of panic at the approach of every vehicle, thinking she was pursued. Three times she had fled to the shelter of a group of wayside cedars, to hide while a wagon lumbered or a car sped by.

Forty-nine, he thought, this is longer than Autobiology or Curious.

Here it is, she gaspt, her breasts rising & falling alarmingly inside a muslin blouse.

He untied the string that was around the portmanteau. In a trice his expert hands held the manuscript.

She lookt at him anxiously as his adept eyes scanned the first few pages. He paid special attention as always to the numbers.

Her body relaxt as she saw that he wanted to continue. She lookt down & saw that her nipples made points visible in the fabric of her blouse. Looking from the side as I always used to at Sylvia M., one could have caught a glimpse of her breast between the buttons. But there was no one there to see.

Stan was happier than he'd expected to be. This book was better than Whirlpool by Diane Giguere. It was better than Knife on the Table by Jacques Godbout. It was even better than Execution by Colin McDougald.

It was a story about a detective who, after following a false lead to a mountaintop in British Columbia, confronts the slayer of Tom Thompson in London Ontario.

She felt her GWG's sticking to her. Well, what do you think, she askt.

We'll apply for a grant in the morning, he replied.

Chapter L

So it was a success story. Canadian literature had succeeded. But if it had succeeded was it really Canadian literature.

Lately they have been pretending that there is a succession in Canadian literature. One of them said there are two main lines in Canadian poetry & I noticed that I'm not in either. This is happening around the Great Lakes & down the St Lawrence River, the same place Canadian history happened.

Remember Stan is from Northern Alberta. He was a little child named Stan & that is funny.

To get into Canadian literature it helps to be a little child named Alec or Ian or Malcolm. Canadian literature like Canadian history is largely Scottish.

Stan had started off with books & now here he was with the Pretty Good Canadian Novel. On the four o'clock Rapido going back to Toronto. It was a mystery to him. It was as if he were under water & there werent any fish there. Just drowned poets & swimming novelists. The hulls of American novels could be seen, dark shapes on the bright surface above.

Stan counted them. He was happier with numbers than with letters.

The train went by Kingston where they were locking the doors on Canadian literature.

The train went by Belleville where a taxi cab floated by the rooftops, startling all the fish.

The train pulled into Toronto. Thomas Wolfe just had time to fill in the last page of his twelfth notebook as the businessmen pickt up their plastic bags full of suits & went out to the taxi cabs on Front Street. Take me straight to Canadian literature, they all said.

Stan walkt to the subway with the novel under his arm & a Doukhobor hat on his head. The Yonge Street stops reminding him of a serial poem.

Across the car from him he saw Robert Fulford reading the Toronto Star. He was reading a column by Robert Weaver. It was about a new Canadian novel by Robert Kroetsch. The subject of the novel was a Scottish-Indian artist named Robert Six Beavers.

It lookt like another great day for Canadian literature in Toronto.

Stan took the portmanteau with him to the press & unwrapt it.

He askt the hip young artistic designer to start working on a cover for the Pretty Good Etcetera.

The latter said I'm way ahead of you, Chief. He went back into the upstairs room where he had six floodlights trained upon the still-wet body of Tom Thompson. Plainly visible was a maple leaf that had become affixt to Tom's Scottish wool sweater.

I dont understand anything about all this said Stan.

I dont either I said. That's why sometimes I hanker for the continuity you observe them maintaining over there at the U.of T.

PART SIX:
The Return of Evangeline

Chapter LI

You might have been wondering why I said hurray for Claire Trevor. Here is why I said hurray for Claire Trevor. Miss Claire Trevor died & went to heaven & came back to earth on a space ship. She came back to earth at Ottawa, Ontario.

The Prime Minister lookt up from the Canadian history he was writing, & he thought he must be dreaming. A space ship on the lawn at 24 Sussex Drive.

But he wasnt dreaming. It was Claire Trevor all right. She walkt toward him, wearing a costume straight out of It Happened One Night.

As I live & breathe, he said, Claire Trevour. I thought you'd gone to heaven.

That's Trevor, without the U, she replied.

I thought you'd gone to heaven, he persisted.

This is heaven nor am I out of it, she purred. Then she leaned suggestively against his chair, as

171

he remembered seeing in The Big Clock.

Is this a science fiction novel, askt the PM.

She smiled. Do I look like a bug-eyed monster, she askt.

He shifted uncomfortably. The air was somehow filled with the sound of suggestive electronic music, long sustained notes in the lower register.

I have come simply as a messenger, she said, from women's heaven.

Women's heaven, he cried. Isnt it all one—

Heavens no, she laught, a man's reach should exceed his grasp or what's a heaven for.

You mean we too, we will be only men? Like a locker room? Like the YMCA?

Sort of like the House of Commons, she said. But I have a message from Evangeline.

Just a minute please, he said, then turned to a seemingly empty chair. Isnt this a kind of hard one to write, he askt.

It sure is, Mr President—

That's Prime Minister.

Yes, Prime Minister, one of the hardest.

Let me tell you, it isnt easy for me either, he said.

Do you want to hear the message or dont you, asked Claire, her face taking on a scowl that revived the memory of Dragonwyck.

The music switcht almost imperceptibly to a half-tone higher. The grass beneath the space ship bent below the force of whatever energy warmed there.

Please, I'm all ears, said the bilingual head of government.

Your mouth is kind of cute too, she simpered.

The message, he implored.

Evangeline wants to come back to Canada. She wants to meet Robert Fulford & somebody called Sparrow, & put her case to them anew.

Put her case to them . . . that wouldnt be Eighteenth Century Louisiana slang, would it, the suspicious & somehow excited Prime Minister suggested.

Give me the right answer to take back to women's heaven with me & you might find out, she said, placing a long cigarette between her full red lips.

Tell her to come by all means, said he.

& when she & her crew had gone he avoided my glance, but he did not return to his writing.

Chapter LIII

Shove over, I want to talk to the reader. I want to say something to the reader reading. Reader reading, dont imagine any more that you can put on your invisibility suit & watch what they are doing, what Jane & Rochester are doing, what they are saying to each other what Evangeline & Fulford are saying to each other.

Either admit that what I report of the matter is the truth of the matter or face the truth, that if you can see them they can see you. Literature is not a one-way mirror. I dont care whether you believe that what I'm telling you is true without my proving it to you or showing it to you in your invisibility suit, or that if you can see them they can see you & what happened to fifty-two, as long as you do one or the other. Writing is not transparent writing is not a window people dont live in three-sided houses like a play by Arthur Miller. Writing is words & you cant see thru words. You cant see thru pictures &

you cant see thru words.

Many a weary year had passt since the burning of Grand-Pré, & while no one was forgiving anything many were forgetting something.

Fulford & Sparrow & the PM were waiting in the afternoon air on the grass at 25 Sussex Drive. They'd gone across the street because the PM's wife didnt want any more scorch marks on her lawn.

Her husband had let a lot of grass grow under his feet & she wanted to keep it that way.

She had come from the foot of Black Mountain & she wasnt going to let that happen again. She was going to grow health food & a mighty oak. This was 1976.

All at once a radiant figure appeared among the three Canadians.

It's okay, John, said the PM, gesturing calmly to his bodyguard hidden in the shadow of the neighbour's tool shed.

Did you say it's a Cajun, this worthy askt in a loud confused voice.

No, he just sneezed, dummy, said Fulford the editor & wry columnist.

The Sparrow remained quiet, biding his time. The words okay John reminded him of Okanagan, & he was furious with himself for having spelled it the American way, with a no.

Calmly & sadly she waited, until the procession approacht her, & she beheld the face of Fulford pale with emotion.

This latter worthy said that he was happy that she was back in her own land & that he was at the moment drafting a column demanding that citizenship he conferred upon her by an act of parliament.

Sparrow spoke up for the first time. He was a short fellow & his words were belligerent as the words of shorties often are.

This is what he said. No no, you small ell liberal, she is not a citizen, she is the figment of an American poet's imagination, & as such is simply another agent of U.S. imperialism.

The PM saw that he would have to lean heavily upon his vaunted powers of compromise.

Chapter LIV

Have you noticed, said one of the characters to another one of the characters, that we characters all talk a lot like the author.

Yes, said Sparrow, but which author are you speaking of or for, are you speaking of Delsing or his American influences, your real creator in more ways than one.

Are you using the word way in its full etymological sense, that is in terms of road, because if you are I know more about ways than you ever will. I've been down that road before.

Fulford admired her grit & the way she spoke up for herself. He had always imagined Marie-Evangeline as an all-suffering Eighteenth Century girl from a minority culture. Now he noticed that she didnt have a left breast. No succor there, he thought, perhaps crudely.

He had always thought of her as a quiet angel, & fixt his eyes upon her as the saint of his deepest devotion. Now here she was fresh out of women's heaven with one tit. He was a little afraid & a little thrilled.

No, said the PM, I dont talk like any author but myself, calice. I make the authors talk the way I do, dont I, Bob.

But Bob wasnt listening to him. He was hearing the bump bump of a pirogue as it nosed its way up the bank of an overgrown swamp.

He was filled with a sense of the injustice of it all. Her head lookt not at all like a vegetable. It reminded him of an innocence forever lost. It reminded him of a tragic Nova Scotian girl he had seen on the stage of the Victory Burlesque.

Footnote, cried the author, I had no idea this was going to enter his mind.

Are we going to get down to brass tax, said Sparrow. I vote that we send this foreign woman back where she came from.

Now that's an interesting point in political philosophy, said the PM. You are it seems aligning yourself with those imperialists who kickt her out of the country to begin with.

You should of stuck to literature, said Fulford, where you belong, fellow.

What about me, said the setting, have you forgotten about setting & landscape. Is it going to be all character & plot & theme.

Not one of the characters heard a word.

Literature is only one of the tools of political & economic aggression, said Sparrow, standing on a stump. This Christian woman has reality only in the poem & the poem is foreign.

Ah, but that is a Black Mountain precept, rejoined Fulford.

A what, askt the PM. Incidentally, as to costume, he was wearing a British hound's tooth jacket over a turtle neck sweater.

Animals all over the place & no body.

I stood up for my rights on Black Mountain said the apparition. It is there that John A. Whatsisname put his hand on my left breast.

But the mood (yeah, that too, said the setting) was shattered.

There was a revolver in Sparrow's left hand!

Chapter LV

By looking along the barrel of the gun & thence along the gunman's arm, to his shoulder, & then over his shoulder across the expanse of real turf to the flowerbed at 24 Sussex Drive, you could see that the PM's gardener employed stakes to hold up the peonies.

None of the four people held up his or her hands. They were, at least the majority of them, too surprised. Indeed they were.

I mean so was I & so were you & you notice they dont even notice you any more. They are suddenly back in a modern instance, most of them.

Damn it, she was beautiful.
& they were so ridiculous there.
I'm ashamed of the whole scene.
I'm tempted to cut out & come back down at 9

Toby Crescent, where the Southern Ontario poets are playing racquet ball on the lawn. Joan, though, is a plant expert, an earth mother, & she is tying peonies to the stakes. Chris is aiming his racquet at the others including Brownie the sky father.

But it wont do. I wont do it, or they wont, they wont do it. That isnt even a novel anyway, but poets at play, a drama. This isnt & I'm not. You thought so but I'm not.

Syrup oozed out of a hole in a maple tree behind Fulford. If Sparrow had fired that would have been where his first shot went, but he hadnt fired. The syrup oozed out & Brian was 2500 miles away, publishing earlier parts of this novel.

Dont do it, said the PM. What do you think I am, the Canada Council.

What do you think this is, another hollow literary jape, said Sparrow. This is the defense of Canada.

That's best left to the army-navy-airforce, said the PM. You are engaged in ultra-left adventurism.

Editorial revisionism, said Fulford. Which reminds me. We usually spell defence with a C up here.

She's going right back, traitors, lackeys of imperialism, running dogs, etc. She's going back to where those who dwell there have named it the Eden of Louisiana.

Jesus, you cant even construct a complex

English sentence, said Fulford. How can you expect to rewrite Canadian Literary History if you cant even handle a dependent clause.

I'm talking about *in*dependence, you rootless cosmopolite, snarled Sparrow. The fellow did have a short temper.

But cant you see that you are acting like the non-Canadians you revile when you pull a gun like that on us, said the PM. Where was that gun made, anyway.

Sparrow had acquired it during his student days below the undependent border when he got all tangled in those initials. Startled for a moment, he glanced at the manufacturer's name on the barrel.

It was then that Evange made her move. All at once there was a bow in her hands, the string pulled back past her chest where the demi-bosom was missing.

She loost the shaft & it flew true, shooting the gun right out of Sparrow's hand.

There. See. That proves it, said Sparrow. She is one of them.

Chapter LVI

But as logical as Sparrow's accusation may have seemed, he was a defeated man, another martyr to cultural determinism.

The PM was a little frightened of her, but nevertheless smitten with the bowsperson.

Fulford thought this was more significant than any movie ever funded by the Canadian Film Development Corporation.

They voted with their hearts & eventually the wronged lady was offered her repatriation. She simply smiled & her erotit weapon disappeared, did you get all of that one. That's more like it, I remember that happening more often earlier before this got all bogged down in plot. Beaten down into ploughshares partaking of the most thematic of rimes.

She smiled yes she did & one knew she was getting ready to leave & me too.

You are looking for a resolution, she said, you

too dislike discontinuity & unrest. A tape with numbers on it, that's what you want, to put around my one breast, the war measures act in the battle of the sexes back in the time where you are.

Come on, said Fulford, that is unnecessarily arch, not classic prose at all, Angel.

The PM said we just want to correct a sad political misdeed of the past, & type thirty at the bottom of another happy story.

But history is an idea of linear time, she said.

Aw, we've heard that one before, said Fulford. What we are really after is to assuage our guilt & bring relief from a national neurosis regarding opprest minorities such as Louis Riel & yourself.

Riel wasnt even a citizen either, said Sparrow, no longer able to contain himself.

The PM spoke to him. This is what he said. Why dont you eat you know what.

In answer to Fulford's statement, the vision replied, you are arguing psychology, & psychology is a system of cyclical time.

What else is there, not counting eternity because here you are said someone else. You might as well know it, it was myself.

Turning to me she said you know because you are mouthing it, there is mythical time. These three easterners are from a text book, they are admythical in short. Myth is a truth of repetitive time. It is a blot that bleeds thru all time.

I bowed my head beneath her point. You are

right, I said. This has all been a waste of time.

Yes, & that is why I love you, she said. I am now, though, forced to choose between you, my forest, & the paradise I have found in women's heaven.

I cannot keep you, my sister, I said between quivering lips that felt many piercings.

No, you are not that. But you are from this day markt.

The others watcht as she stood on tiptoe momentarily to kiss me in front of my brain, then walkt swiftly to her craft & disappeared from her audience.

I swore on the spot to do the same.

Thirty.

(Vancouver, July 1975 — July 1976)

INDEX

189

TALONBOOKS — FICTION IN PRINT 1977

Songs My Mother Taught Me — Audrey Thomas
Blown Figures — Audrey Thomas
Hungry Hills — George Ryga
Theme for Diverse Instruments — Jane Rule
Mrs. Blood — Audrey Thomas
Night Desk — George Ryga
Ballad of a Stonepicker — George Ryga
Durer's Angel — Marie-Claire Blais
A Short Sad Book — George Bowering
Desert of the Heart — Jane Rule
The Schoolmarm Tree — Howard O'Hagan
The Woman Who Got on at Jasper Station — Howard O'Hagan